This book belongs to

....

....

THE
PUFFIN TREASURY
of
STORIES

THE
PUFFIN TREASURY
of
STORIES

Edited by Judith Elkin

PUFFIN

PUFFIN BOOKS
Published by the Penguin Group
Penguin Books Ltd, 80 Strand, London WC2R 0RL, England
Penguin Group (USA) Inc., 375 Hudson Street, New York, New York 10014, USA
Penguin Group (Canada), 90 Eglinton Avenue East, Suite 700, Toronto, Ontario, Canada M4P 2Y3
(a division of Pearson Penguin Canada Inc.)
Penguin Ireland, 25 St Stephen's Green, Dublin 2, Ireland (a division of Penguin Books Ltd)
Penguin Group (Australia), 250 Camberwell Road, Camberwell, Victoria 3124, Australia
(a division of Pearson Australia Group Pty Ltd)
Penguin Books India Pvt Ltd, 11 Community Centre, Panchsheel Park, New Delhi - 110 017, India
Penguin Group (NZ), cnr Airborne and Rosedale Roads, Albany, Auckland 1310, New Zealand
(a division of Pearson New Zealand Ltd)
Penguin Books (South Africa) (Pty) Ltd, 24 Sturdee Avenue, Rosebank, Johannesburg 2196, South Africa

Penguin Books Ltd, Registered Offices: 80 Strand, London WC2R 0RL, England

penguin.com

First published as *The Puffin Twentieth-Century Collection of Stories* by Puffin Books 1999
This edition published by Puffin 2006
1 3 5 7 9 10 8 6 4 2

This edition copyright © Penguin Books Ltd, 1999 and 2006
All illustrations remain the copyright © of the individual illustrators credited, 1999
The acknowledgements on page 180 constitute an extension of this copyright page

The moral right of the illustrators has been asserted

Printed in China

British Library Cataloguing in Publication Data
A CIP catalogue record for this book is available from the British Library
ISBN-13: 978–0–141–38324–8
ISBN-10: 0–141–38324–0

CONTENTS

JACQUELINE WILSON

FROM *Double Act*

ILLUSTRATED BY NICK SHARRATT

If our writing's a bit shaky, it's because we're doing this account in the van.

We feel shaky. Our whole lives have been shaken up.

Dad really has bought a bookshop! He didn't even take us with him to check it out first. He went away for the weekend with Rose, and when he came back he said, 'Guess what! I've bought a shop!'

We just stared at him, stunned. He's been acting so crazy. Not like a dad at all. Especially not our dad.

We're used to him saying, 'Guess what! I've bought another box of books.'

But you don't buy a book*shop* just like that. You're meant to hang around for months, getting it surveyed and seeing solicitors.

'It's all simple,' said Dad. 'This sweet old couple are retiring and are happy to move out straightaway. If I can't sell our own house, I'll let it out to students for a bit. Your gran's got her sheltered flat all worked out. Rose only rents her room, and she can shut up her stall in the arcade any time, so she hasn't got any problems either.'

We're the ones with the problems. Garnet and me.

We don't even get considered.

'Why didn't you take us with you to see if *we* like it?' I said.

'You'll love it,' said Dad. 'The village is right out in the country, beside

a river, with hills all around. It's a real story-book place. There's a pond with puddleducks straight out of Beatrix Potter. There's just this one street of shops. Ours is in the middle. We'll fit it out with shelves and Rose can have the window for her bric-a-brac. She's got all sorts of ideas for getting it done up. And there's plenty of room upstairs. You two can have the attic for your bedroom – you'll like that.'

Sarah Crewe gets stuck in an attic in A Little Princess *and she has to act like a servant to all the girls in her school. Though at least she got to stay in her school.*

We've had to leave our school.
It was awful saying goodbye.
But it was much worse saying goodbye to

Ruby doesn't want to write it. She always leaves the worst bit to me. I don't want to write it either.

Oh, Gran. We do miss you. We miss you ever so ever so much. You used to get cross and you were strict and sometimes you even smacked, but you didn't hurt because of your poor hands and you couldn't help being strict because you're old and you were only cross when we were naughty.

But we do so wish you were with us now. You could be cross and strict and smack all the time and we wouldn't mind a bit.

You didn't get cross and strict and smack when we took you to your new flat. But you weren't all happy and smiley. You looked so small and scrunched up and sad and it was so awful.

We helped you put your chair and your china cabinet and all the rest of your stuff in your new room, but they didn't look right. They didn't look yours. It didn't look like a home.

This funny old man next door came round to say hello and he gave you a bunch of flowers he'd grown in his garden. Dad teased and said you'd got yourself a boyfriend already, but you wouldn't smile. And when Dad said he hoped you'd be really happy in your new flat and he was sure it was all for the best, you just sniffed. You didn't say anything, but you looked at Dad and it was as if you were shrieking: Who are you kidding?

You didn't even kiss Dad properly goodbye, just gave him your cheek. And we don't blame you either, Gran.

You kissed us. And we kissed you. Lots and lots.

We didn't talk to Dad either. We're still not speaking to him properly. Or Rose. We don't need to. We can just speak to each other. In Twinspeak, so they can't understand.

Garnet and I have this special language. We've got heaps of made-up words for things. Sometimes we don't use words at all, we use signs. Little tiny things like widening our eyes or putting our heads slightly to one side. We signal to each other and then both start up a pretend

coughing fit or sneeze simultaneously or shriek with manic laughter.

Rose isn't used to this. It doesn't half make her jump.

'Pack it in,' says Dad.

I glance at Garnet.

'Pack it in what, Dad?' we say simultaneously.

'Less of the cheek,' says Dad, taking one hand off the steering wheel and swatting at us.

'How do they *do* that?' Rose asks.

'How do we do what?' we say.

'Stop it! You're giving me the creeps. Can you really read each other's thoughts?' she says, shivering.

'Of course they can't,' says Dad.

'Then how can they say the same thing at the same time in that weird way?' Rose says, peering at us.

'I don't know,' says Dad, shrugging.

'*We* know,' we say, and we raise our eyebrows and make our eyes glitter in a mysterious and mystic manner.

We wait until Rose turns round again and starts fiddling with the old van radio, trying to tune it to a station. I point to it and nudge Garnet. We both start singing loudly, our timing spot on.

Rose gasps.

'Cut it out, twins,' says Dad sharply.

I turn my fingers into pretend scissors and make lots of cutting movements. Garnet does the same.

'Oh, very funny,' says Dad, not at all amused.

When he's concentrating on the road, I change the scissors to a dagger and mime a sudden bloody attack on Rose. Garnet does likewise, only she's not quite quick enough. Dad sees, so Garnet shakes her arm quickly, making out she's got cramp.

'What are you playing at, you two?' says Dad.

We blink at him and shrug.

Dad sighs with exasperation, and then takes one hand off the steering wheel and puts his arm round Rose.

I nudge Garnet and we both make a very rude noise.

Dad's hand tightens on Rose's shoulder, but he doesn't say anything. She doesn't say anything either. Neither do we. The radio keeps buzzing and fading and going funny.

I feel a bit like that too. Maybe I'm starting to feel car-sick. Well, van-sick. Ooh good, if I'm going to throw up then I shall aim at Rose.

SYLVIA WAUGH

FROM *The Mennyms*

ILLUSTRATED BY PETER BAILEY

It was ten o'clock in the evening when Soobie struggled through the front door supporting Appleby, who was leaning on him like a dead weight. His coat was wet, his umbrella was torn and his boots were covered in mud. But his discomforts were nothing compared to Appleby's.

Tulip and Vinetta had rushed together to answer the door-bell. They brought the wanderers in out of the cold, rainy night into the comfortably heated hall. Soobie quickly removed his wet coat and dirty boots and put his ruined umbrella in the cloakroom.

Then they all concentrated upon Appleby. Her beautiful red hair was matted with mud and looked no colour at all. Her sweatshirt and jeans were caked with dirt. She had somehow managed to lose her shoes and her socks were in shreds. Her green eyes looked unseeing and lustreless. They were obviously nothing but green buttons, sewn in place by Kate forty years ago. Whatever magic had turned them into functioning eyes had gone. Only the mouth remained alive, turned down at the edges and quivering.

Vinetta looked shocked. All the things she might have said, the reproaches she might have made, the explanations she might have demanded, remained unspoken. When Appleby slumped forward, Vinetta caught her in her arms and hugged her tight till the murky water that had penetrated her whole body began to ooze out. Tulip and Scoobie helped to take her into the lounge and they laid her down on the settee.

The mouth still quivered but nothing else moved.

'What shall we do?' Vinetta asked Tulip, looking terrified.

Tulip looked at her filthy grand-daughter and her distraught daughter-in-law.

'She will have to have a bath in one of the big baths,' she said decisively. 'All that dirt has gone deep into her system. Sponging or even showering will not get it out.'

The green buttons flickered to life for a moment. Appleby looked horrified. But she had not the strength to protest, or even to maintain her look of horror for long.

Vinetta was worried. No one had ever had a bath. A sponge down, yes. Even a very quick dive into and out of the shower. But a bath?

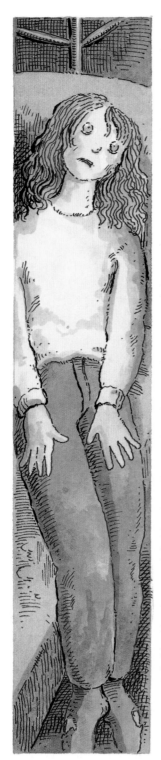

'Are you sure, Tulip?' she asked doubtfully. 'The water will go right through her. We'll never be able to get her dry again.'

Tulip's crystal eyes looked hard and determined, like a doctor who knows his insistence upon drastic surgery is risky but right.

'There is water inside her now,' she explained '– filthy water. She looks to me as if she's fallen into a pond. We must get the dirt out and then think about how to dry her afterwards.'

On the settee, Appleby lay stretched out and lifeless. Dirty water was dripping from every part of her. Her face, hands, and all of her clothing were covered in slime. Bits of green weed were clinging to her. She looked not just wet but drowned.

'There is no life left in her,' said Vinetta as she timidly touched her daughter's arm. 'It would be cruel to put her to any more torment. Let her rest.'

'No,' insisted Tulip, 'we must be cruel to be kind. There will never be life in her till she is clean and dry. If she is allowed to dry off in the state she is in now, she will dry stiff and solid and goodness knows what problems that would lead to.'

'How do we know that she'll ever come to life again?' asked Vinetta, but even as she asked it she remembered the head, limbs and torso they had found in the attic. They had become Pilbeam, and Pilbeam was as alive as any of them.

'We don't know,' replied Granny Tulip brusquely, 'but we have nothing to lose by trying.'

Soobie had stood by silent, considering what was

said. Then he put his weight behind his grandmother's wisdom.

'We'll have to carry her up to the bathroom on the first floor. We can fill the bath with warm water and put some shampoo into it. Whatever we wash dries. Our hair dries. Our clothes dry. So though it may take longer and be more difficult, you can depend on it, Appleby will dry.'

She was heavy. My goodness, she was heavy! They lugged her up the stairs and into the bathroom. They sat her on a chair whilst the bath was being prepared. Soobie, having helped with the heavy work, left his mother and grandmother to get on with the business of washing.

Since every bit of Appleby was made of cloth, it did not occur to them to remove the dirty sweatshirt and jeans. Only the tattered socks were pulled off ready to throw in the rubbish. When the bath was felt to be of a suitable depth and temperature, Appleby was plunged into it. The soapy water soon turned black and scummy.

Vinetta fetched a scrubbing brush from the kitchen and scrubbed away at her daughter's hair, face, arms, jeans, sweatshirt, everything. After half an hour, Appleby was, if possible, wetter than at first, her body soaking up the water like a sponge, but she was not much cleaner.

'Pull out the plug,' ordered Tulip, trying to stay calm, but by no means sure that the remedy she had prescribed was going to work.

The dirty water drained away leaving a broad,

black tidemark round the bath, and slumped inside it, a dazed, grey figure making feeble efforts to move arms and legs.

'She's still moving,' said Tulip, feeling frightened but trying to sound hopeful.

'What next?' asked Vinetta with a tinge of anger in her voice.

They tried to lift Appleby out of the bath, but she was too heavy.

'Get Soobie,' ordered Tulip. 'We'll take her to the bathroom upstairs and run another bath, but before we put her into it, we'll rinse the dirty suds off under the shower up there.'

Soobie, Vinetta and Tulip dragged Appleby up the next flight of stairs, over the beautiful blue Durham carpet.

'The carpet's getting filthy,' said Soobie.

'Never mind the carpet,' snapped Vinetta. 'That's easily seen to.' She was almost out of breath and fully out of patience.

As the suds were washed away under the shower, Appleby began to look a normal colour again. Her face was turning pinkish. Her hair was back to its natural shade of red. The green sweatshirt was still streaked with dirt, but recognisably green. The jeans were nearly clean and Appleby's feet and ankles showed beneath in flesh-coloured hues with toe-nails painted red, though the paint was chipped and the toes were still greyish.

'She has toe-nails!' exclaimed Tulip, and then on closer inspection, she added, in a voice of disapproval, 'and she paints them!'

Appleby still could not speak but she gave her grandmother a withering look as much as to say, 'They're my toenails and I'll do what I like with them.'

'Into the bath with you,' said Tulip as she and Vinetta tipped her into the clean water. This time the suds did not go grey and the scrubbing brush stayed white. After a final ducking under the shower, Appleby looked almost normal.

Almost, but not quite. Her limbs and torso, full of water, looked

bloated. Her cheeks were abnormally plump so that the green button eyes were almost lost in their folds. She was dazed. Her movements, oh yes she was still moving, were slow and laboured. She looked like a spaceman. She still could not speak.

'Soobie,' said Tulip, 'go and take the shelves out of the empty airing cupboard.'

Soobie went next door and quickly removed all the slats that formed the two shelves and stacked them in a corner on the landing.

In the meantime, Vinetta and Tulip together, using four very large bath-towels, dried Appleby's hair and squeezed as much water as they could out of her limbs. Soon the towels were saturated, but, except for her hair, Appleby looked just as wet as ever.

'Now,' said Tulip when Soobie returned, 'fetch Appleby's basket chair from her room, and another couple of bath-towels from downstairs. Put the towels on the airing cupboard floor and the chair on top of them.'

By now, they had the terrified Appleby sitting on the bathroom stool, one either side supporting her. When Soobie had done his job, he helped the two women to manoeuvre his sister into the chair in the cupboard. Tulip explained to the dazed girl what was happening.

'You can sit here in the warm till you dry out. Go to sleep. No one will disturb you. It may take a week or two, but you must get completely dry. That is all you have to do. We'll look in on you from time to time to see how you are doing. I'll bring you my little brass bell. If you want anything, you can ring it.'

Oh, there were levels upon levels to that speech! Practical it was, and helpful. But Tulip was really putting on the biggest pretend of her life. She was pretending desperately that this bizarre situation was just a bit of ordinary, everyday life. And at another level, she had a quiet, malicious satisfaction in thinking that this adolescent, who had caused so much trouble, would be stuck in a cupboard for a considerable time to think over her misdeeds.

'You will be all right?' asked Vinetta diffidently, longing to take Appleby in her arms and make it all better there and then, but knowing that such instant relief was beyond reach.

Appleby gave her mother a look of cool resignation. The pretend had just about worked. She could almost believe that, given time, everything might be all right. And, to be truthful, she was longing for them to close the door and leave her to recover, or even to die, alone.

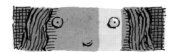

ANNE FINE

FROM *Flour Babies*

ILLUSTRATED BY GEORGE SMITH

Simon sat across the kitchen table from his flour baby and gave her a poke.

The flour baby fell over.

'Ha!' Simon scoffed. 'Can't even sit up yet!'

He set the flour baby up again, and gave her another poke. Again, she fell over.

'Not very good at standing up for yourself, are you?' Simon taunted, setting her up again.

The flour·baby fell over backwards this time, off the table into the dog basket.

'Blast!'

'You mustn't swear in front of it,' Simon's mother said. 'You'll set it a terrible example.'

Simon reached down to scoop the flour baby off Macpherson's cushion, and picked the dog's hairs off her frock.

'Not *it*,' he reproved his mum in turn. '*Her*.'

She was definitely a her. Definitely. Some of the flour babies Mr Cartright had handed out that morning could have been one or the other. It wasn't clear. But not the one that landed in Simon's lap.

'Catch, Dozy! Aren't you supposed to be one of the school's sporting heroes? Wake up!'

She was *sweet*. She was dressed in a frilly pink bonnet and a pink nylon frock, and carefully painted on her sacking were luscious sexy round eyes fringed with fluttering lashes.

Robin Foster, beside him, was jealous instantly.

'How come you get one with eyes? Mine's just plain sacking. Do you want to swap?'

Simon tightened his grip round his flour baby.

'No. She's mine. You paint eyes on your own if you want them.'

'And yours has clothes!' He turned to yell at Mr Cartright, who was just coming to the end of tossing bags of flour round the room. 'Sir! Sir! Sime's dolly has got a frock and a bonnet and eyes and everything. And mine's got nothing. It's not fair.'

'If every parent who had a baby who was a bit lacking sent it back,' Mr Cartright said, 'this classroom would be practically empty. Sit down and be quiet.'

He heaved himself up on the desk, and started reading the rules of the experiment.

FLOUR BABIES

(1) The flour babies must be kept clean and dry at all times. All fraying, staining and leakage of stuffing will be taken very seriously indeed.

(2) Flour babies will be put on the official scales twice a week to check for any weight loss that might indicate casual neglect or maltreatment, or any weight gain that might indicate tampering or damp.

(3) No flour baby may be left unattended at any time, night or day. If you *must* be out of sight of your flour baby, even for a short time, a responsible babysitter must be arranged.

(4) You must keep a Baby Book, and write in it daily. Each entry should be no shorter than three full sentences, and no longer than five pages.

(5) Certain persons (who shall not be named until the experiment is over) shall make it their business to check on the welfare of the flour babies and the keeping of the above rules. These people may be parents, other pupils, or members of staff or the public.

He looked up.
'That's it.'

He'd never seen a class reduced to silence before. An interesting sight. You had to hand it to Dr Feltham and these boffin types. They had weird powers. Some of them might fumble in and out of the staffroom, letting their woollies unravel behind them, and visibly having to trawl through their memory banks each time someone asked them if they took sugar in their tea. But they could work wonders. They could wreak miracles. With their mysterious arts, they could do the unimaginable. They could blow the whole planet to smithereens. They could silence 4C.

'Well?' he asked, somewhat unnerved. 'Any questions?'

Simon picked up his flour baby and lifted her frock. No knickers, unless you counted sacking bag. Already she had black smudges on her bum where he'd sat her on the pen runnel of the double desk along which Robin Foster's rubber dropping collection had recently overflowed.

'Now look at that,' he complained to Robin. 'She's already dirty, and it's your fault, Foster. You're going to have to keep this desk a whole lot cleaner in future.'

Robin stared down at the little heaps of filthy rubbing-out scurf, assiduously kept so he and Simon would always have raw material for flicking pellets. Then he glanced at Simon, trying to work out if he had been joking. Finally, from the quiver of possible responses, he chose the sharpest arrow: ridicule.

'Sir! Sir!' he'd yelled, his fist punching the air as he called for the whole room's attention. 'You've got to move me, sir. I can't stay here. It's not safe. Sime Martin's turning into my mother!'

They kept the joke up for the rest of the day. By the time the last bell rang, Simon was absolutely sick of having to prop his flour baby carefully on top of his book bag, then go after whoever it was who'd last called him Old Mrs Martin, or Mother Sime, and bash their head hard against the wall. By the time he shambled out of the back gate at half past three, his knuckles were burning and his wrist badly grazed. He only stopped himself wiping the blood off on the flour baby's frock because, through some miracle, he heard the echo of his mother's voice ring out of nowhere in his ears: 'Oh, no, Simon! Not blood! It's the *worst*!' He wiped his hand clean down his shirt instead.

And now here was his mother in the flesh, spooning out more free advice.

'You ought to put it in a plastic bag. Keep it clean.'

'Is that what you did with me?'

His mother laughed as she dumped his supper down in front of him. Egg and beans.

'I wish I'd had the sense.'

She was joking, he supposed. But still, it was a thought. Having him must have made all the difference. He'd come along, a whole other person to be taken into account. Real, too. Not just something like a flour baby that could be shoved in a plastic bag to be kept clean, without fetching up on some murder charge. When had she realized how much trouble he was going to be? Some pennies took time to drop. He himself could still remember the day, not that long ago, when he'd first realized he was a person.

He'd been having it out with a turkey. Behind the caravan park where Simon and his mother went on holiday there was a farm, and one of the larger turkeys had pushed its bad-tempered, gobbling way through the fence and was giving Simon the eye – well, first one eye then the other – and stopping him getting to the lavatories.

Simon got his own back the simplest way he could.

'Christmas!' he jeered. 'Din-dins!'

The turkey gobbled off. But Simon had to sit on the lavatory steps for a moment. He'd suddenly realized that by Christmas Day the turkey would really be dead on a plate, but (barring the sort of daft accidents his mother was always going on about), he, Simon, would still be alive.

And somehow that set him off thinking. He pulled the flesh on the back of his hand up into a miniature tent, and then let go. The skin sprang back instantly, keeping him in shape. His shape. It struck Simon for the first time in his life that he was totally unique. In the whole history of the universe, there had never been one of him before. There would never be another.

'Not a very nice place to sit.'

Someone was stepping over him to get to the urinals. But Simon, off on another tack, scarcely heard. Once, only a few years ago, Simon *wasn't* – didn't exist at all. And one day, like that turkey, he wouldn't exist again. Ever.

'Can't you find somewhere a bit more *salubrious* to sit?'

The same fellow again, on his way out. Simon paid no attention, his mind on other things. Hadn't he just discovered himself – him – the one and only Sime Martin, alive, and (unlike the turkey) knowing it?

From that day on, Simon had looked at himself with a whole new respect, a far greater interest. The other holiday-makers became almost accustomed to seeing the lad from the end plot contorting himself into odd shapes, not like the family near the showerhuts who did yoga, but simply in order to gaze at parts of his body he'd never really looked at properly before: heels, elbows, belly button, inner thighs.

'God knows which bits of himself he stares at in private!'

'Do you suppose the poor boy's *mental*?'

'It's his mother I feel sorry for really.'

'Do stop that, Simon! People will think you've got *lice*.'

Neither the neighbours' whispered comments nor his mother's sharp orders grazed Simon's consciousness. He was busy. Busy probing his huge, lank body with a curiosity, a real wonder, he'd never felt before. All that went through his brain was 'This is *me*'. But there was more to it than that, much more, though he could never have explained it, and, in the intervening years, no one had ever asked him.

He had a question for his mother now, though. Picking the last of Macpherson's wiry hairs off the flour baby, he asked:

'What was I like?'

His mother sucked a stray bean off her fingertip.

'When?'

'When I was a baby.'

Simon's mother narrowed her eyes at him across the table. Give a boy a dolly, she thought, sighing inwardly, and he goes all broody within minutes. What hope is there for girls?

But it was a fair question, and he hadn't asked it for a good few years.

Her son deserved an honest answer.

'You were *sweet*,' she said. 'Good as gold, and chubby as a bun, and you had bright button eyes. You were so lovely that perfect strangers kept stopping the pram in the street to coo at you and tell me how lucky I was to have you. Everybody wanted to blow raspberries on your tummy. No doubt about it, you were the most beautiful baby in the world.'

He knew she wouldn't want him to spoil things by saying it, but he couldn't help himself.

'So why did my dad push off so quickly?'

His mother tried her usual tack of making a joke of the whole business.

'Be fair, Simon. He did hang around for six whole weeks!'

But she could tell from the look on his face that the answer wasn't working the way it usually did. So she tried throwing in her Old Crone imitation.

'And there be those who say he could see into the future . . .'

TERRY PRATCHETT

FROM *Diggers*

ILLUSTRATED BY PAUL BIRKBECK

Everything was going well. Or, at least, not very badly.

Oh, there was still plenty of squabbling and rows between the various families, but that was nomish nature for you. That's why they'd set up the Council, which seemed to be working. Nomes liked arguing. At least the Council of Drivers meant they could argue without hardly ever hitting one another.

Funny thing, though. Back in the Store the great departmental families had run things. But now all the families were mixed up and, anyway, there were no departments in a quarry. But by instinct, almost, nomes liked hierarchies. The world had always been neatly divided between those who told people what to do, and those who did it. So, in a strange way, a new set of leaders was emerging.

The Drivers.

It depended on where you had been during the Long Drive. If you were one of the ones who had been in the lorry cab, then you were a Driver. All the rest were just Passengers. No one talked about it much. It wasn't official or anything. It was just that the bulk of nomekind felt that anyone who could get the Truck all the way here was the sort of person who knew what they were doing.

Being a Driver wasn't necessarily much fun.

Last year, before they'd found the Store, Masklin had to hunt all day.

Now he only hunted when he felt like it; the younger Store nomes liked hunting and apparently it wasn't *right* for a Driver to do it. They mined potatoes and there'd been a big harvest of corn from a nearby field, even after the machines had been round. Masklin would have preferred them to grow their own food, but the nomes didn't seem to have the knack of making seeds grow in the rock-hard ground of the quarry. But they were getting fed, that was the main thing.

Around him he could feel thousands of nomes living their lives. Raising families. *Settling down.*

He wandered back to his own burrow, down under one of the derelict quarry sheds. After a while he reached a decision and pulled the Thing out of its own hole in the wall.

None of its lights were on. They wouldn't do that until it was close to electricity wires, when it would light up and be able to talk. There were some in the quarry, and Dorcas had got them working. Masklin hadn't taken the Thing to them, though. The solid black box had a way of talking that always made him unsettled.

He was pretty certain it could hear, though.

'Old Torrit died last week,' he said after a while. 'We were a bit sad but, after all, he was very old and he just died. I mean, nothing ate him first or ran him over or anything.'

Masklin's little tribe had once lived in a motorway embankment beside rolling countryside which was full of things that were hungry for fresh nome. The idea that you could die simply of not being alive any more was a new one to them.

'So we buried him up on the edge of the potato field, too deep for the plough. The Store nomes haven't got the hang of burial yet, I think. They think he's going to sprout, or something. I think they're mixing it up

with what you do with seeds. Of course, they don't know about growing things. Because of living in the Store, you see. It's all new to them. They're always complaining about eating food that comes out of the ground; they think it's not natural. And they think the rain is a sprinkler system. I think *they* think the whole world is just a bigger Store. Um.'

He stared at the unresponsive cube for a while, scraping his mind for other things to say.

'Anyway, that means Granny Morkie is the oldest nome,' he said eventually. 'And *that* means she's entitled to a place on the Council even though she's a woman. Abbot Gurder objected to that but we said, all right, you tell her, and he wouldn't, so she is. Um.'

He looked at his fingernails. The Thing had a way of listening that was quite off-putting.

'Everyone's worried about the winter. Um. But we've got masses of potatoes stored up, and it's quite warm down here. They've got some funny ideas, though. In the Store they said that when it was Christmas Fayre time there was this thing that came called Santer Claws. I just hope it hasn't followed us, that's all. Um.'

He scratched an ear.

'All in all, everything's going right. Um.'

He leaned closer.

'You know what that means? If you think everything's going right, something's going wrong that you haven't heard about yet. That's what I say. Um.'

The black cube managed to look sympathetic.

'Everyone says I worry too much. I don't think it's *possible* to worry too much. Um.'

He thought some more.

'Um. I think that's about all the news for now.' He lifted the Thing up and put it back in its hole.

He'd wondered whether to tell it about his argument with Grimma, but that was, well, personal.

It was all that reading books, that was what it was. He shouldn't have let her learn to read, filling her head with stuff she didn't need to know. Gurder was right, women's brains *did* overheat. Grimma's seemed to be boiling hot the whole time, these days.

He'd gone and said, look, now everything was settled down more, it was time they got married like the Store nomes did, with the Abbot muttering words and everything.

And she'd said, she wasn't sure.

So he'd said, it doesn't work like that, you get told, you get married, that's how it's done.

And she'd said, not any more.

He'd complained to Granny Morkie. You'd have expected some support there, he thought. She was a great one for tradition, was Granny. He'd said: Granny, Grimma isn't doing what I tell her.

And *she'd* said: Good luck to her. Wish I'd thought of not doin' what I was told when I was a gel.

Then he'd complained to Gurder who said, yes, it was very wrong, girls should do what they were instructed. And Masklin had said, right then, you tell her. And Gurder had said, well, er, she's got a real temper on her, perhaps it would be better to leave it a bit and these were, after all, changing times.

Changing times. Well, that was true enough. Masklin had done most of the changing. He'd had to make people think in different ways to leave the Store. Changing was necessary. Change was right. He was all in favour of change.

What he was dead against was things not staying the same.

His spear was leaning in the corner. What a pathetic thing it was . . .

now. Just a bit of flint held on to the shaft with a twist of binder twine. They'd brought saws and things from the Store. They could use metal these days.

He stared at the spear for some time. Then he picked it up and went out for a long, serious think about things and his position in them. Or, as other people would have put it, a good sulk.

★

The old quarry was about halfway up the hillside. There was a steep turf slope above it, which in turn became a riot of bramble and hawthorn thicket. There were fields beyond.

Below the quarry a lane wound down through scrubby hedges and joined the main road. Beyond that there was the railway, another name for two long lines of metal on big wooden blocks. Things like very long trucks went along it sometimes, all joined together.

The nomes had not got the railway fully worked out yet. But it was obviously dangerous, because they could see a lane that crossed it and, whenever the railway moving thing was coming, two gates came down over the road.

The nomes knew what gates were for. You saw them on fields, to stop things getting out. It stood to reason, therefore, that the gates were to stop the railway from escaping from its rails and rushing around on the roads.

Then there were more fields, some gravel pits – good for fishing, for the nomes who wanted fish – and then there was the airport.

Masklin had spent hours in the summer watching the planes. They drove along the ground, he noticed, and then went up sharply, like a bird, and got smaller and smaller and disappeared.

That was the *big* worry. Masklin sat on his favourite stone, in the rain that was starting to fall, and started to worry about it. So many things were worrying him these days he had to stack them up, but below all of them was this big one.

They should be going where the planes went. That was what the Thing had told him, when it was still speaking to him. The nomes had come from the sky. Up above the sky, in fact, which was a bit hard to understand, because surely the only thing above the sky was more sky. And they should go back. It was their . . . something beginning with D. Density. Their density. Worlds of their own, they once had. And somehow they'd got stuck here. But – this was the worrying part – the ship thing, the aeroplane that flew through the really high sky, between the stars, was still up there somewhere. The first nomes had left it behind when they came down here in a smaller ship, and it had crashed, and they hadn't been able to get back.

And he was the only one that knew.

The old Abbot, the one before Gurder, he had known. Grimma and Dorcas and Gurder all knew some of it, but they had busy minds and they were practical people and there was so much to organize these days.

It was just that everyone was settling down. We're going to turn this into our little world, just like in the Store, Masklin realized. They thought the roof was the sky, and we think the sky is the roof.

We'll just stay and . . .

There was a truck coming up the quarry road. It was such an unusual sight that Masklin realized he had been watching it for a while without really seeing it at all.

'There was no one on watch! Why wasn't there anyone on watch? I said there should always be someone on watch!'

Half a dozen nomes scurried through the dying bracken towards the quarry gate.

'It was Sacco's turn,' muttered Angalo.

'No, it wasn't!' hissed Sacco. 'You remember, yesterday you asked me to swap because –'

'I don't care whose turn it was!' shouted Masklin. 'There was no one there! And there should have been! Right?'

'Sorry, Masklin.'

'Yeah. Sorry, Masklin.'

They scrambled up a bank and flattened themselves behind a tuft of dried grass.

It was a small truck, as far as trucks went. A human had already

climbed out of it and was doing something to the gates leading into the quarry.

'It's a Land Rover,' said Angalo smugly. He'd spent a long time in the Store reading everything he could about vehicles, before the Long Drive. He liked them. 'It's not really a truck, it's more to carry humans over –'

'That human is sticking something on the gate,' said Masklin.

'On *our* gate,' said Sacco disapprovingly.

'Bit odd,' said Angalo. The man sleepwalked, in the slow, ponderous way that humans did, back to the vehicle. Eventually it backed around and roared off.

'All the way up here just to stick a bit of paper on the gate,' said Angalo, as the nomes stood up. 'That's humans for you.'

Masklin frowned. Humans were big and stupid, that was true enough, but there was something unstoppable about them and they seemed to be controlled by bits of paper. Back in the Store a piece of paper had said the Store was going to be demolished and, sure enough, it *had* been demolished. You couldn't trust humans with bits of paper.

He pointed to the rusty wire netting, an easy climb for an agile nome.

'Sacco,' he said, 'you'd better fetch it down.'

Miles away, *another* piece of paper fluttered on the hedge. Spots of rain pattered across its sun-bleached words, soaking the paper until it was heavy and soggy and . . .

. . . tore.

It flopped on to the grass, free. A breeze made it rustle.

JENNY NIMMO

FROM *The Snow Spider*

ILLUSTRATED BY SIÂN BAILEY

He waited until his grandmother had settled herself in the armchair and sipped her tea before he knelt beside her and took out the matchbox. He wanted her undivided attention for his revelation. Even so he was unprepared for the ecstatic gasp that accompanied Nain's first glimpse of the spider, when he gently withdrew the lid. The tiny creature crawled on to his hand, glowing in the dark room, and Nain's eyes sparkled like a child's. 'How did it come?' Her whisper was harsh with excitement.

'In the snow,' Gwyn replied. 'I thought it was a snowflake. It was the brooch, I think. I gave it to the wind, like you said, and this . . . came back!'

'So,' Nain murmured triumphantly, 'you are a magician then, Gwydion Gwyn, as I thought. See what you have made!'

'But did I make it, Nain? I believe it has come from somewhere else. Some far, far place . . . I don't know, beyond the world, I think.'

'Then you called it, you brought it here, Gwydion Gwyn. Did you call?'

'I did but . . .' Gwyn hesitated, 'I called into

the snow, the names you said: Math, Lord of Gwynedd, Gwydion and Gilfaethwy. Those were the only words.'

'They were the right words, boy. You called to your ancestors. The magicians heard your voice and took the brooch to where it had to go, and now you have the spider!'

Nain took the spider from Gwyn and placed it on her arm. Then she got up and began to dance through the shadowy wilderness of her room. The tiny glowing creature moved slowly up her purple sleeve, until it came to her shoulder, and there it rested, shining like a star beneath her wild black curls.

Gwyn watched and felt that it was Nain who was the magician and he the enchanted one.

Suddenly his grandmother swooped back and, taking the spider from her hair, put it gently into his hands. 'Arianwen,' she said. 'White silver! Call her Arianwen; she must have a name!'

'And what now?' asked Gwyn. 'What becomes of Arianwen? Should I tell about her? Take her to a museum?'

'Never! Never! Never!' said Nain fiercely. 'They wouldn't understand. She has come from another world to bring you closer to the thing you want.'

'I want to see my sister,' said Gwyn. 'I want things the way they were before she went.'

Nain looked at Gwyn through half-closed eyes. 'It's just the beginning, Gwydion Gwyn, you'll see. You'll be alone, mind. You cannot tell. A magician can have his heart's desire if he truly wishes it, but he will always be alone.' She propelled her grandson gently but firmly towards the door. 'Go home now or they'll come looking, and never tell a soul!'

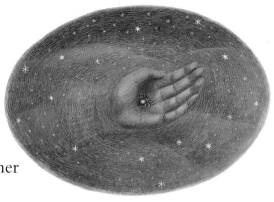

★

The farmhouse was empty
when Gwyn reached home.
Mr Griffiths could be heard
drilling in his workshop. Mrs
Griffiths had popped out to see
a neighbour, leaving a note for her
son on the kitchen table,

'SOUP ON THE STOVE.
STOKE IT UP IF IT'S COLD.'

'The soup or the stove?' Gwyn muttered to himself. He opened the
stove door, but the red embers looked so warm and comforting he was
reluctant to cover them with fresh coal. He turned off the light and
knelt beside the fire, holding out his hands to the warmth.

He must have put the matchbox down somewhere and he must have
left it open, because he suddenly became aware that Arianwen was
climbing up the back of the armchair. When she reached the top she
swung down to the arm, leaving a silver thread behind her. Up she
went to the top, and then down, her silk glistening in the firelight.
Now the spider was swinging and spinning back and forth across the
chair so fast that Gwyn could only see a spark, shooting over an ever-
widening sheet of silver.

'A cobweb!' he breathed.

And yet it was not a cobweb. There was someone there. Someone
was sitting where the cobweb should have been. A girl with long pale
hair and smiling eyes: Bethan, sitting just as she used to sit, with her legs
tucked under her, one hand resting on the arm of the chair, the other
supporting her chin as she gazed into the fire. And still Arianwen spun,
tracing the girl's face, her fingers and her hair, until every feature

became so clear Gwyn felt he could have touched the girl.

The tiny spider entwined the silk on one last corner and then ceased her feverish activity. She waited, just above the girl's head, allowing Gwyn to contemplate her creation without interruption.

Was the girl an illusion? An image on a silver screen? No, she was more than that. Gwyn could see the impression her elbow made on the arm of the chair, the fibres in her skirt, the lines on her slim, pale hand.

Only Bethan had ever sat thus. Only Bethan had gazed into the fire in such a way. But his sister was dark, her cheeks were rosy, her skin tanned golden by the wind. This girl was fragile and so silver-pale she might have been made of gossamer.

'Bethan?' Gwyn whispered, and he stretched out his hand towards the girl.

A ripple spread across the shining image, as water moves when a stone pierces the surface, but Gwyn did not notice a cool draught entering the kitchen as the door began to open.

'Bethan?' he said again.

The figure shivered violently as the door swung wider, and then the light went on. The girl in the cobweb hovered momentarily and gradually began to fragment and to fade until Gwyn was left staring into an empty chair. His hands dropped to his side.

'Gwyn! What are you doing, love? What are you staring at?' His mother came round the chair and looked down at him, frowning anxiously.

Gwyn found that speech was not within his power. Part of his strength seemed to have evaporated with the girl.

'Who were you talking to? Why

were you sitting in the dark?' Concern caused Mrs Griffiths to speak sharply.

Her son swallowed but failed to utter a sound. He stared up at her helplessly.

'Stop it, Gwyn! Stop looking at me like that! Get up! Say something!' His mother shook his shoulders and pulled him to his feet.

He stumbled over to the table and sat down, trying desperately to drag himself away from the image in the cobweb. The girl had smiled at him before she vanished, and he knew that she was real.

JILL PATON WALSH

FROM *Gaffer Samson's Luck*

ILLUSTRATED BY TIM CLAREY

He woke in the moonlight, suddenly knowing what to do. 'I'll do that when you've done it,' he had said to Terry. And Terry had done it; the rules didn't say you had to succeed, only that you mustn't funk it. So now it was up to James. Earlier in the day he had been terrified of the weir; now he knew there were worse things, and he had a choice. His father often said, talking about climbing and fell-walking, that people got into trouble because they rushed at things, and didn't take time to think. So James took time to think. He sat in the pool of moonlight on the attic floor, and thought about the weir. He thought of the rush of water, knee-deep, or deeper, the slack chain, the slimy sill beneath. Then he got his climbing boots out of the cupboard. The row of heavy studs on the soles glinted in the cold silver light.

Now. It would have to be now. Tomorrow the flood might have gone down a bit, the fierceness of the weir abated. But if he did it the same day, the same night, there could be no arguing about it. James looked out of the window. The world was dim, but clear. Shadow spires stood into a faint sky. A bright full moon was shining in a cloudless night, littered with brilliant stars. Just the same, he would need a torch. He crept about barefoot, finding his clothes. He had to retrieve his jeans from the airing cupboard, where his mother had put them to dry. He took a boot in each hand, and crept down the stairs.

His bike was still propped on the fence beside the lock; he would have to walk. He tiptoed across the gravel, for fear the crunch would wake someone. In the street he sat on the kerb beneath a lamp-post, and put on his boots, and laced them up. Then he set off for the trailer park.

Angey woke easily; one or two taps on the pane, and there she was, yawning, and dressed. Now he came to think of it, she looked as if she slept in her clothes.

'You don't have to,' she said, at once.

'Yes, I do,' he said. 'But I need someone to see me, or they'll never believe us. Can you get someone?'

She nodded. 'I'll get my trainers, and I'll be right with you,' she said.

They went to Tracy's house first. Angey thought Tracy slept downstairs, but they woke an angry dog before they woke her. Next they tried Ted. James thought wistfully of Scarf, but Scarf was kept in hospital, Angey said. She threw a light handful of grit at Ted's window, and in a while he put his head out. 'Coming,' he said when he saw

them, but seemed to take hours. James got desperate, waiting for him.

'I can't wait, Angey,' he said. 'I've just got to go and do it. Bring anyone you can, OK?'

The road through the village under the tall trees was dark. The lamp-posts were still on, but the limited dim pools of light they made failed to meet

each other. James had no idea what time it was, he hadn't brought his watch. No point in wrecking a good watch. He picked his way by torchlight between the pools of lamplight. His boots rang and clattered on the road. And he felt like a thief going by; anyone who saw him would stop him. At last he crossed the bridge, thudding over the planks, and came into the open, gleaming meadow. Threads of silver, broken shards of moon lay in the ghostly grass. He marched on regardless through the pools on the path, to the bank. He did not look at the lock, he couldn't afford to. Hearing the solid roar of the river through it was bad enough. As he crossed the first weir he couldn't help looking where the water ran as hard as ever, leaping and shouting to the distant and disinterested stars. And then he trudged through the bushes, and was there.

The river gave off a steely glint as it curved over the slope. Were the chains hanging just above the water instead of just into it? James dared not consider now, or stop to think. Instead he turned his back on the river, and lowered himself into the water, going in very deliberately on the riverward side of the chain.

He had expected more depth; it came up to his knees, no more. He had not expected the weight and force of its thrust. It was so cold his skin burned intensely, he felt the violent flushing of his body all over, but he was hanging on to the first post. He felt for the sill, the concrete edge below the water, and carefully hooked the first row of studs on his boots over the lip. He picked up the chain, lifted it over his shoulders, and leaned back into it, pushing against the thrust of the water. Then he began very slowly, holding himself rigid and leaning backwards with all his might to slide sideways.

As long as he kept leaning against the weight of the water, as long as he didn't let it push him forward, and topple him over the chain, he would be all right. The warm flush of his skin ebbed away leaving him trembling and gasping from cold. Somehow he had eased himself

along the first length of chain. As he moved towards the middle it got harder, and he leaned back so far he was looking straight up at the icy stars. He got to the second post. Then he found he couldn't move; he was clinging on to it frantically, terrified of going on, and terrified of going back while his mind replayed to him the sight of Terry being plucked off the chain and flung away. 'But you can't stay,' he told himself. 'You'll get tired, and get washed off, so *move!*' Slowly he unclenched the grip of his right hand, and transferred it to the next length of chain.

He was right in the middle of the weir now, hanging on to the central chain, and fighting for his balance. The water was immense, ruthless. It pushed him forward, and he fought with all the thrust in his frozen limbs to keep himself leaning away from the water-slide, to keep his boots locked over the sill, while the water roared round his knees, and tried to tear his feet from under him. He slid his boots along the sill; he reached the next post. Above the sound of the water, faintly, something reached him; bird-like sounds, voices, calling. He had no mind to spare for that. Somewhere between the third and fourth posts he lost his footing; the sill was crumbling and rough, and he couldn't slide his boots along it. For a moment he teetered, closed his eyes, and gave up. His body flinched all over at the thought of the drubbing and knocking it would take, being dashed down into the pool; and then

somehow he had recovered his posture, and was leaning outwards in
the loop of chain again. And the force of the water was lessening now
with every step he took. He was reaching the lee of the other shore.

The water sped past this length, and turned sideways moments later
as though it did not know at first that it was free to go over. Even so,
James, suddenly aching and mortally tired, hardly managed the last few
steps to the bank. And there he hung on, leaning on the last post, and
barely able to drag his soaking body out of the water, and roll himself
on to the bank.

Dimly he heard shouting. His name, being called. He looked back across the shining terrifying moon-silvered stretch of water. Like a solitary glow-worm the torch was dancing. Someone had found it lying on the bank, and was waving it. The shadows in the willows on the other side, moved, and called his name. Lots of shadows. Angey had brought the whole village mob out to watch him.

DICK KING-SMITH

FROM *The Sheep-Pig*

ILLUSTRATED BY MICHAEL TERRY

Fly ran left up the slope as the sheep began to bunch above her. Once behind them, she addressed them in her usual way, that is to say sharply.

'Move, fools!' she snapped. 'Down the hill. If you know which way "down" is,' but to her surprise they did not obey. Instead they turned to face her, and some even stamped, and shook their heads at her, while a great chorus of bleating began.

To Fly sheep-talk was just so much rubbish, to which she had never paid any attention, but Babe, listening below, could hear clearly what was being said, and although the principal cry was the usual one, there were other voices saying other things. The contrast between the politeness with which they had been treated by yesterday's rescuer and the everlasting rudeness to which they were subjected by this or any wolf brought mutinous thoughts into woolly heads, and words of defiance rang out.

'You got no manners! . . . Why can't you ask nicely? . . . Treat us like muck, you do!' they cried, and one hoarse voice which the pig recognized called loudly, 'We don't want you, wolf! We want Babe!' whereupon they all took it up.

'We want Babe!' they bleated. 'Babe! Babe! Ba-a-a-a-abe!'

Those behind pushed at those in front, so that they actually edged a

pace or two nearer the dog.

For a moment it seemed to Babe that Fly was not going to be able to move them, that she would lose this particular battle of wills; but he had not reckoned with her years of experience. Suddenly, quick as a flash, she drove in on them with a growl and with a twisting leap sprang for the nose of the foremost animal; Babe heard the clack of her teeth as the ewe fell over backwards in fright, a fright which immediately ran through all. Defiant no longer, the flock poured down the hill, Fly snapping furiously at their heels, and surged wildly through the gateway.

'No manners! No manners! No ma-a-a-a-a-nners!' they cried, but an air of panic ran through them as they realized how rebellious they had been. How the wolf would punish them! They ran helter-skelter into the middle of the paddock, and wheeled as one to look back, ears pricked, eyes wide with fear. They puffed and blew, and Ma's hacking cough rang out. But to their surprise they saw that the wolf had dropped by the gateway, and that after a moment the pig came trotting out to one side of them.

Though Farmer Hogget could not know what had caused the near-revolt of the flock, he saw clearly that for some reason they had given Fly a hard time, and that she was angry. It was not like her to gallop sheep in that pellmell fashion.

'Steady!' he said curtly as she harried the rear-guard, and then 'Down!' and 'Stay!' and shut the gate. Shepherding suited Farmer Hogget – there was no waste of words in it.

In the corner of the home paddock nearest to the farm buildings was a smallish fenced yard divided into a number of pens and runways. Here the sheep would be brought at shearing-time or to pick out fat lambs for market or to be treated for various troubles. Farmer Hogget had heard the old ewe cough; he thought he would catch her up and give her another drench. He turned to give an order to Fly lying flat and still behind him, and there, lying flat and still beside her, was the pig.

'Stay, Fly!' said Hogget. And, just for fun, 'Come, Pig!'

Immediately Babe ran forward and sat at the farmer's right, his front trotters placed neatly together, his big ears cocked for the next command.

Strange thoughts began to stir in Farmer Hogget's mind, and unconsciously he crossed his fingers.

He took a deep breath, and, holding it . . . 'Away to me, Pig!' he said softly.

Without a moment's hesitation Babe began the long outrun to the right.

Quite what Farmer Hogget had expected to happen, he could never afterwards clearly remember. What he had not expected was that the pig would run round to the rear of the flock, and turn to face it and him, and lie down instantly without a word of further command spoken, just as a well-trained dog would have done. Admittedly, with his jerky little rocking-horse canter he took twice as long to get there as Fly would have, but still, there he was, in the right place, ready and waiting. Admittedly, the sheep had turned to face the pig and were making a great deal of noise, but then Farmer Hogget did not know, and Fly would not listen to, what they were saying. He called the dog to heel, and began to walk with his long loping stride to the collecting-pen in the corner. Out in the middle of the paddock there was a positive babble of talk.

'Good morning!' said Babe. 'I do hope I find you all well, and not too distressed by yesterday's experience?' and immediately it seemed that every sheep had something to say to him.

'Bless his heart!' they cried, and, 'Dear little soul!' and, 'Hullo, Babe!' and, 'Nice to see you again!' and then there was a rasping cough and the sound of Ma's hoarse tones.

'What's up then, young un?' she croaked. 'What be you doing here instead of that wolf?'

Although Babe wanted, literally, to keep on the right side of the sheep, his loyalty to his foster-mother made him say in a rather hurt voice, 'She's not a wolf. She's a sheep-dog.'

'Oh all right then,' said Ma, 'sheep-dog, if you must have it. What dost want, then?'

Babe looked at the army of long sad faces.

'I want to be a sheep-pig,' he said.

'Ha ha!' bleated a big lamb standing next to Ma. 'Ha ha ha-a-a-a-a!'

'Bide quiet!' said Ma sharply, swinging her head to give the lamb a thumping butt in the side. 'That ain't nothing to laugh at.'

Raising her voice, she addressed the flock.

'Listen to me, all you ewes,' she said, 'and lambs too. This young chap was kind to me, like I told you, when I were poorly. And I told him, if he was to ask me to go somewhere or do something, politely, like he would, why, I'd be only too delighted. We ain't stupid, I told him, all we do want is to be treated right, and we'm as bright as the next beast, we are.'

'We are!' chorused the flock. 'We are! We are! We a-a-a-a-a-are!'

'Right then,' said Ma. 'What shall us do, Babe?'

Babe looked across towards Farmer Hogget, who had opened the gate of the collecting-pen and now stood leaning on his crook, Fly at his feet. The pen was in the left bottom corner of the paddock, and so Babe expected, and at that moment got, the command 'Come by, Pig!' to send him left and so behind the sheep and thus turn them down towards the corner.

He cleared his throat. 'If I might ask a great favour of you,' he said hurriedly, 'could you all please be kind enough to walk down to the gate where the farmer is standing, and to go through it? Take your time, please, there's absolutely no rush.'

A look of pure contentment

passed over the faces of the flock, and with one accord they turned and walked across the paddock, Babe a few paces in their rear.

Sedately they walked, and steadily, over to the corner, through the gate, into the pen, and then stood quietly waiting. No one broke ranks or tried to slip away, no one pushed or shoved, there was no noise or fuss. From the oldest to the youngest, they went in like lambs.

Then at last a gentle murmur broke out as everyone in different ways quietly expressed their pleasure.

'Babe!' said Fly to the pig. 'That was quite beautifully done, dear!'

'Thank you so much!' said Babe to the sheep. 'You did that so nicely!'

'Ta!' said the sheep. 'Ta! Ta! Ta-a-a-a-a-a! 'Tis a pleasure to work for such a little gennulman!' And Ma added, 'You'll make a wunnerful sheep-pig, young un, or my name's not Ma-a-a-a-a-a.'

As for Farmer Hogget, he heard none of this, so wrapped up was he in his own thoughts. He's as good as a dog, he told himself excitedly, he's better than a dog, than any dog! I wonder . . .!

'Good Pig,' he said.

Then he uncrossed his fingers and closed the gate.

PENELOPE LIVELY

FROM *The Ghost of Thomas Kempe*

ILLUSTRATED BY GEORGE SMITH

It was tacked to the wooden frame of the notice-board with a rusty nail. Almost before James had read it he knew what was coming. The writing was larger this time, and the letters rather more carefully formed. It was obviously intended to be a notice, or, more precisely, an advertisement. It said:

For the discoverie of goodes loste by the crystalle or by booke and key or with the sieve & sheeres seeke me at my dwellynge which lyes at the extremetie of East Ende Lane. I have muche skille also in such artes as alchemie, astronomie etc. & in physicke & in the seekynge out of wytches & other eville persons. My apprentice, who dwells at the same howse, will bring me messages.

It was signed, rather flamboyantly, with much swirl and flourish:
Thos. Kempe Esq. Sorcerer.

'There!' said James, with a mixture of triumph and despair. 'There! Now do you believe me?'

Simon took his glasses off, scrubbed round them with his fingers and read the notice for a second time. 'Well,' he said cautiously.

'Well what?'

'Somebody could have put it there.'

'Such as who?'

'I don't know.'

'Such as me, perhaps?' said James in a freezing voice.

'No. Not you. You've been with me all morning. You know something?'

James didn't answer.

'If anyone sees it,' Simon went on amiably, 'they might sort of connect it with you. Because it mentions your house.'

James' anger gave way to alarm. 'What shall I do?'

Simon glanced up and down the street. There was no one in sight. The police-station windows stared blankly down at them.

'Take it off. Quickly.'

James hesitated. Then he darted forward, tweaked the notice from the nail and began to walk quickly away down the road, stuffing it in his pocket. Simon caught him up.

'Let's have another look.'

Pulling the notice out again, James saw with indignation that his own red biro had been used once more, and a page from his exercise book. He tore it into very small pieces and put it in a litter basket by the bus stop.

'Whoever he is, this person,' said Simon, 'he's got some pretty funny ideas, hasn't he? Jiggery-pokery with sieves and whatnot to find out who stole things. He'd make a pretty rotten policeman. And leaves for medicines and all that. It wouldn't work – not now there's penicillin and things.'

'He just wants things done like they were in his time,' said James.
'With him doing them. And me helping.'

'Oh,' said Simon. 'I see.' He sounded very polite. Too polite.

James said, 'You don't believe he's a ghost, do you?'

'I didn't say I didn't.'

'But you don't.'

'I kind of half do and half don't,' said Simon with great honesty. 'I
do when I'm with you but I think if I was by myself I wouldn't.'

They walked on for a few minutes in silence. Then Simon said,
'What are you going to do? I mean, whatever it is or whoever it is he
keeps getting you into trouble.'

'I know. And I'm getting fed up with it. What *can* I do?'

'If he is — what you think,' said Simon, 'there's one thing you could
try.'

'What?'

'Ask him to stop it.'

James stared. 'Talk back to him?'

'That's it. Worth trying anyway.'

'Yes. I s'pose it might be.' Somehow that had not occurred to him.
But, when you stopped and thought about it, there was no reason why
this should be a one way conversation. If he was here, this Thos.
Kempe, Sorcerer, making a right nuisance of himself, then the best
thing might well be to talk straight back at him. Maybe that was all
that was needed. Just explain quietly and firmly that this sort of thing
really wouldn't do, and he'd see reason and go away. Back where he
came from, wherever that might be.

Feeling rather more hopeful about the future James parted from
Simon at his gate and went home for lunch.

A feeling of dissatisfaction hovered around the house. Mrs Harrison
was suffering one of her attacks of hay-fever, which made her red-eyed
and irritable. Mr Harrison had fallen over a bucket of water standing

in the porch, and was resignedly mopping up the mess as James arrived. He followed James into the kitchen, carrying bucket and cloth, which he dumped down by the sink.

'I don't want to interfere with the housekeeping arrangements,' he said, 'but I must point out that the best place for a full bucket of water is not the centre of the front porch.'

'Not guilty,' said his wife, sneezing violently. 'Must have been a child. And don't talk to me about water. I think I'm about to melt as it is.' She began peeling potatoes, with vicious stabs.

'I've only just come in, haven't I?' said James.

'Good gracious!' said Mr Harrison. 'You don't imagine I'd ever suspect it might have been you, do you?' James gave him a suspicious look and went out into the garden to make sure Helen hadn't been interfering with his hole. He found that Tim had located a tributary to the original rat-hole in the drain, and had spent a happy morning digging up a clump of irises. James hastily re-planted them: Tim never seemed to understand that he was only living with them on sufferance as it was and might one day go too far. Mr Harrison had several times said darkly, 'That dog will have to go.'

James patted him kindly. 'You didn't know they weren't weeds, did you?' he said. 'Like you couldn't know Dad still wanted that pair of slippers. Lucky thing I found where you'd buried them, eh?' Tim dropped his head slightly, and bared his teeth in a kind of pink grin, which was the nearest he came to a gesture of affection. He wasn't one of those dogs who climb all over you. He had dignity.

'Come here, sir,' said James sternly. He saw himself and Tim, suddenly, as an intrepid team of criminal trackers: Harrison of the Yard and his famous trained Rumanian Trufflehound, the Burglar's Scourge. He began to slink along the side of the house with a ferocious scowl on his face, towing a reluctant Tim by the collar. On the other side of that drainpipe lurked the notorious Monte Carlo Diamond Gang, armed to the teeth . . .

'Lunch!' shouted Mrs Harrison from the scullery window. Tim shook himself free and bolted for the back door.

After lunch the pewter clouds that had been slowly massing above the village all morning opened up into determined, continuous rain. Mrs Harrison said she felt as though she was being drowned from without as well as within, and went to bed with a book. Mr Harrison went to sleep in an armchair. Helen went to see a friend.

James remembered he had some homework to do. He climbed up to his bedroom, closed the door, and sat down at his table. Tim padded round the room once or twice, jumped up on the bed, swirled the covers around several times until he achieved a satisfactory position, and went to sleep. Outside, the rain drummed on the roof and poured

in oily rivers down the window.

James opened his project book, looked at his notes, and began to write. It was a project about ancient Greece, and he was enjoying it. He looked things up, and wrote, and stuck some pictures in, and thought about Alexander the Great, and drew a picture of a vase with blokes having a battle on it, and forgot about everything except what he was doing. Around him, the room rustled occasionally: a piece of paper floated to the floor, and a pen rolled across the table. Tim twitched in his sleep.

All of a sudden something nudged James' foot. It was a sheet from his exercise book. He picked it up and read:

I am glad to see thee at thy studies, though I lyke not thy bookes. Where is thy Latin? & where are thy volumes of Astrologie? But to our businesse . . . I have putt out the water for people to knowe wee are seeking thieves: it will doe for a crystalle. Thy father's baldnesse could be stayed by bathing with an ointment made from the leaves of Yarrow (a herb of Venus) but there is no cure for thy mother's ailmente of the eyes for it is caused by wytcherie. Nothing will suffice save to seeke out the wytch & bring her to justice. This muste wee doe with all haste.

James swung round in his chair. Then he got up and searched the room, even looking under the bed. There was nothing to be seen, and nothing moved.

He read the note again. The reference to his father's baldness he found particularly annoying. That was cheek, that was. In fact, he thought, he's a proper busybody, that's what he is.

And then he remembered Simon's suggestion. All right then, let's have a go. Let's try talking to him.

He cleared his throat, feeling distinctly foolish at addressing the empty room, even though there was no one to hear, and said 'Er – Mr Kempe.'

Silence. Tim uncurled himself and looked up, yawning.

James took a deep breath and said firmly, 'I'm afraid I can't do the things you want me to do because people don't go in much for sorcery nowadays. I don't think they'd really be very interested. You see we don't use those kind of medicines now because we've got penicillin and that and we've got policemen for finding out if anyone's pinched things and catching 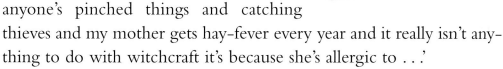 thieves and my mother gets hay-fever every year and it really isn't anything to do with witchcraft it's because she's allergic to . . .'

There was a loud crash behind him. He whirled round. One of his clay pots had fallen on to the floor and smashed. Even as he looked, a second one raised itself from the shelf, flew across the room, narrowly missing his right ear, and dashed itself against the opposite wall. Tim leapt from the bed and rushed about the room, barking furiously.

'Hey! Stop that!' shouted James.

A gust of wind swept wildly round the room, lifting all the papers on the table and whirling them about the floor. The ink-bottle scuttered to the edge of the table and hung there till James grabbed hold of it with one hand while with the other he made ineffectual dabs at the flying pages from his project book.

'Here! Lay off! Cut it out!'

The door opened and banged itself shut again, twice.

The windows rattled as though assaulted by a sudden thunderstorm. The calendar above the bed reared up, twitched itself from the hook, and flapped to the floor. A glass of water on the bedside table tipped

over and broke, making a large puddle on the mat. Downstairs, James could hear the sitting-room door open, and his father's footsteps across the hall.

'Please!' he squeaked breathlessly, using one hand to steady the chair, which was bucking about like a ship in a storm, while with the other he warded off Volume 1 of *A Child's Encyclopaedia* which had risen from the bookshelf and hurled itself at his head.

'Please! Don't! Look, perhaps I could . . .'

Mrs Harrison's bedroom door opened and her voice could be heard saying something loud and not very friendly on the landing. Mr Harrison was coming up the stairs.

The bedcover whisked off the bed, whirled round once or twice, and sank to the floor, engulfing a frantic Tim in its folds.

'All right!' shouted James. 'All right! I'll do it. Anything. If you stop.'

The room subsided. Tim struggled out from under the bedcover and dived for the shelter of the bed. The door opened and Mr Harrison came in. James stood amid the wreckage of his room and waited for the storm to break.

RICHARD ADAMS

FROM *Watership Down*

ILLUSTRATED BY DIZ WALLIS

Hazel turned his head and looked down the course of the brook. Far away, between the two copses, he could see the cherry tree where two days before he had sat with Blackberry and Fiver in the sunrise. He remembered how Bigwig had chased Hawkbit through the long grass, forgetting the quarrel of the previous night in the joy of their arrival. He could see Hawkbit running towards him now and two or three of the others – Silver, Dandelion and Pipkin. Dandelion, well in front, dashed up to the gap and checked, twitching and staring.

'What is it, Hazel? What's happened? Fiver said –'

'Bigwig's in a wire. Let him alone till Blackberry tells us. Stop the others crowding round.'

Dandelion turned and raced back as Pipkin came up.

'Is Cowslip coming?' said Hazel. 'Perhaps *he* knows –'

'He wouldn't come,' replied Pipkin. 'He told Fiver to stop talking about it.'

'Told him *what*?' asked Hazel incredulously. But at that moment Blackberry spoke and Hazel was beside him in a flash.

'This is it,' said Blackberry. 'The wire's on a peg and the peg's in the ground – there, look. We've got to dig it out. Come on – dig beside it.'

Hazel dug once more, his fore-paws throwing up the soft, wet soil

and slipping against the hard sides of the peg. Dimly, he was aware of the others waiting near by.

After a time he was forced to stop, panting. Silver took his place, and was followed by Buckthorn. The nasty, smooth, clean, man-smelling peg was laid bare to the length of a rabbit's ear, but still it did not come loose. Bigwig had not moved. He lay across the wire, torn and bloody, with closed eyes. Buckthorn drew his head and paws out of the hole and rubbed the mud off his face.

'The peg's narrower down there,' he said. 'It tapers. I think it could be bitten through, but I can't get my teeth to it.'

'Send Pipkin in,' said Blackberry. 'He's smaller.'

Pipkin plunged into the hole. They could hear the wood splintering under his teeth – a sound like a mouse in a shed wainscot at midnight. He came out with his nose bleeding.

'The splinters prick you and it's hard to breathe, but the peg's nearly through.'

'Fiver go in,' said Hazel.

Fiver was not long in the hole. He, too, came out bleeding.

'It's broken in two. It's free.'

Blackberry pressed his nose against Bigwig's head. As he nuzzled him gently the head rolled sideways and back again.

'Bigwig,' said Blackberry in his ear, 'the peg's out.'

There was no response. Bigwig lay still as before. A great fly settled on one of his ears. Blackberry thrust at it angrily and it flew up, buzzing, into the sunshine.

'I think he's gone,' said Blackberry. 'I can't feel his breathing.'

Hazel crouched down by Blackberry and laid his nostrils close to Bigwig's, but a light breeze was blowing and he could not tell whether there was breath or not.

The legs were loose, the belly flaccid and limp. He tried to think of what little he had heard of snares. A strong rabbit could break his neck in a snare. Or had the point of the sharp wire pierced the wind-pipe?

'Bigwig,' he whispered, 'we've got you out. You're free.'

Bigwig did not stir. Suddenly it came to Hazel that if Bigwig was dead – and what else could hold *him* silent in the mud? – then he himself must get the others away before the dreadful loss could drain their courage and break their spirit – as it would if they stayed by the body. Besides, the man would come soon. Perhaps he was already coming, with his gun, to take poor Bigwig away. They must go; and he must do his best to see that all of them – even he himself – put what had happened out of mind, for ever.

'My heart has joined the Thousand, for my friend stopped running today,' he said to Blackberry, quoting a rabbit proverb.

'If only it were not Bigwig,' said Blackberry. 'What shall we do without him?'

'The others are waiting,' said Hazel. 'We have to stay alive. There has to be something for them to think about. Help me, or it will be more than I can do.'

He turned away from the body and looked for Fiver among the rabbits behind him. But Fiver was nowhere to be seen and Hazel was afraid to ask for him, in case to do so should seem like weakness and a need for comfort.

'Pipkin,' he snapped, 'why don't you clean up your face and stop the bleeding? The smell of blood attracts elil. You know that, don't you?'

'Yes, Hazel. I'm sorry. Will Bigwig —'

'And another thing,' said Hazel desperately. 'What was it you were telling me about Cowslip? Did you say he told Fiver to be quiet?'

'Yes, Hazel. Fiver came into the warren and told us about the snare, and that poor Bigwig —'

'Yes, all right. And then Cowslip —?'

'Cowslip and Strawberry and the others pretended not to hear. It was ridiculous, because Fiver was calling out to everybody. And then as we were running out Silver said to Cowslip, "Surely you're coming?" And Cowslip simply turned his back. So then Fiver went up and spoke to him very quietly, but I heard what Cowslip answered. He said, "Hills of Inlé, it's all one to me where you go. You hold your tongue." And then he struck at Fiver and scratched his ear.'

'I'll kill him,' gasped a low, chilling voice behind them. They all leapt round. Bigwig had raised his head and was supporting himself on his fore-paws alone. His body was twisted and his hind-parts and back legs still lay along the ground. His eyes were open, but his face was such a fearful mask of blood, foam, vomit and earth that he looked more like some demon-creature than a rabbit. The immediate sight of him, which should have filled them with relief and joy, brought only terror. They cringed away and none said a word.

'I'll kill him,' repeated Bigwig, spluttering through his fouled whiskers and clotted fur. 'Help me, rot you! Can't anyone get this stinking wire off me?' He struggled, dragging his hind-legs. Then he fell again and crawled forward, trailing the wire through the grass with the broken peg snickering behind it.

'Let him alone!' cried Hazel, for now they were all pressing forward to help him. 'Do you want to kill him? Let him rest! Let him breathe!'

'No, not rest,' panted Bigwig. 'I'm all right.' As he spoke he fell again and immediately struggled up on his fore-paws as before. 'It's my back legs. Won't move. That Cowslip! I'll kill him!'

'Why do we let them stay in that warren?' cried Silver. 'What sort of rabbits are they? They left Bigwig to die. You all heard Cowslip in the burrow. They're cowards. Let's drive them out — kill them! Take the warren and live there ourselves!'

'Yes! Yes!' they all answered. 'Come on! Back to the warren! Down with Cowslip! Down with Silverweed! Kill them!'

'*0 embleer Frith!*' cried a squealing voice in the long grass.

At this shocking impiety, the tumult died away. They looked about them, wondering who could have spoken. There was silence. Then, from between two great tussocks of hair-grass came Fiver, his eyes blazing with a frantic urgency. He growled and gibbered at them like a witch-hare and those nearest to him fell back in fear. Even Hazel could not have said a word for his life. They realized that he was speaking.

'The warren? You're going to the warren? You fools! That warren's nothing but a death-hole! The whole place is one foul elil's larder! It's snared – everywhere, every day! That explains everything: everything that's happened since we came here.'

He sat still and his words seemed to come crawling up the sunlight, over the grass.

'Listen, Dandelion. You're fond of stories, aren't you? I'll tell you one – yes, one for El-ahrairah to cry at. Once there was a fine warren on the edge of a wood, overlooking the meadows of a farm. It was big, full of rabbits. Then one day the white blindness came and the rabbits fell sick and died. But a few survived, as they always do. The warren became almost empty. One day the farmer thought, "I could increase those rabbits: make them part of my farm – their meat, their skins. Why should I bother to keep rabbits in hutches? They'll do very well where they are." He began to shoot all elil – lendri, homba, Stoat, owl. He put out food for the rabbits, but not too near the warren. For his purpose they had to become accustomed to going about in the fields and the wood. And then he snared them – not too many: as many as he wanted and not as many as would frighten them all away or destroy the warren. They grew big and strong and healthy, for he saw to it that they had all of the best, particularly in winter, and nothing to fear – except the running knot in the hedge-gap and the wood-path. So they lived as he wanted them to live and all the time there were a few who disappeared.

The rabbits became strange in many ways, different from other rabbits. They knew well enough what was happening. But even to themselves they pretended that all was well, for the food was good, they were protected, they had nothing to fear but the one fear; and that struck here and there, never enough at a time to drive them away. They forgot the ways of wild

rabbits. They forgot El-ahrairah, for what use had they for tricks and cunning, living in the enemy's warren and paying his price? They found out other marvellous arts to take the place of tricks and old stories. They danced in ceremonious greeting. They sang songs like the birds and made shapes on the walls; and though these could help them not at all, yet they passed the time and enabled them to tell themselves that they were splendid fellows, the very flower of Rabbitry, cleverer than magpies. They had no Chief Rabbit – no, how could they? – for a Chief Rabbit must be El-ahrairah to his warren and keep them from death: and here there was no death but one, and what Chief Rabbit could have an answer to that? Instead, Frith sent them strange singers, beautiful and sick like oak-apples, like robins' pin-cushions on the wild rose. And since they could not bear the truth, these singers, who might in some other place have been wise, were squeezed under the terrible weight of the warren's secret until they gulped out fine folly – about dignity and acquiescence, and anything else that could make believe that the rabbit loved the shining wire. But one strict rule they had; oh yes, the strictest. No one must ever ask where another rabbit was and anyone who asked, "Where?" – except in a song or a poem – must be silenced. To say "Where?" was bad enough, but to speak openly of the wires – that was intolerable. For that they would scratch and kill.'

He stopped. No one moved. Then, in the silence, Bigwig lurched to his feet, swayed a moment, tottered a few steps towards Fiver and fell again. Fiver paid him no heed but looked from one to another among the rabbits. Then he began speaking again.

'And then *we* came, over the heather in the night. Wild rabbits, making scrapes across the valley. The warren rabbits didn't show themselves at once. They needed to think what was best to be done. But they hit on it quite soon. To bring us into the warren and tell us nothing. Don't you see? The farmer only sets so many snares at a time and if one rabbit dies, the others will live that much longer. You suggested that Hazel should tell them our adventures, Blackberry, but it didn't go down well, did it? Who wants to hear about brave deeds when he's ashamed of his own, and who likes an open, honest tale from someone he's deceiving? Do you want me to go on? I tell you, every single thing that's happened fits like a bee in a foxglove. And kill them, you say, and help ourselves to the great burrow? We shall help ourselves to a roof of bones, hung with shining wires! Help ourselves to misery and death!'

Fiver sank down into the grass. Bigwig, still trailing his horrible, smooth peg, staggered up to him and touched his nose with his own.

'I'm still alive, Fiver,' he said. 'So are all of us. You've bitten through a bigger peg than this one I'm dragging. Tell us what to do.'

'Do?' replied Fiver. 'Why, go – now. I told Cowslip we were going before I left the burrow.'

'Where?' said Bigwig. But it was Hazel who answered.

'To the hills,' he said.

TED HUGHES

FROM *The Iron Man*

ILLUSTRATED BY CHRIS RIDDELL

The Iron Man came to the top of the cliff.

How far had he walked? Nobody knows. Where had he come from? Nobody knows. How was he made? Nobody knows.

Taller than a house, the Iron Man stood at the top of the cliff, on the very brink, in the darkness.

The wind sang through his iron fingers. His great iron head, shaped like a dustbin but as big as a bedroom, slowly turned to the right, slowly turned to the left. His iron ears turned, this way, that way. He was hearing the sea. His eyes, like headlamps, glowed white, then red, then infra-red, searching the sea. Never before had the Iron Man seen the sea.

He swayed in the strong wind that pressed against his back. He swayed forward, on the brink of the high cliff.

And his right foot, his enormous iron right foot, lifted up, out, into space, and the Iron Man stepped forward, off the cliff, into nothingness.

CRRRAAAASSSSSSSH!

Down the cliff the Iron Man came toppling, head over heels.

CRASH!

CRASH!

CRASH!

From rock to rock, snag to snag, tumbling slowly. And as he crashed and crashed and crashed

His iron legs fell off.

His iron arms broke off, and the hands broke off the arms.

His great iron ears fell off and his eyes fell out.

His great iron head fell off.

All the separate pieces tumbled, scattered, crashing, bumping, clanging, down on to the rocky beach far below.

A few rocks tumbled with him.

Then

Silence.

Only the sound of the sea, chewing away at the edge of the rocky beach, where the bits and pieces of the Iron Man lay scattered far and wide, silent and unmoving.

Only one of the iron hands, lying beside an old, sand-logged washed-up seaman's boot, waved its fingers for a minute, like a crab on its back. Then it lay still.

While the stars went on wheeling through the sky and the wind went on tugging at the grass on the cliff-top and the sea went on boiling and booming.

Nobody knew the Iron Man had fallen.

Night passed.

Just before dawn, as the darkness grew blue and the shapes of the rocks separated from each other, two seagulls flew crying over the rocks. They landed on a patch of sand. They had two chicks in a nest on the cliff. Now they were searching for food.

One of the seagulls flew up – Aaaaaark! He had seen something. He glided low over the sharp rocks. He landed and picked something up.

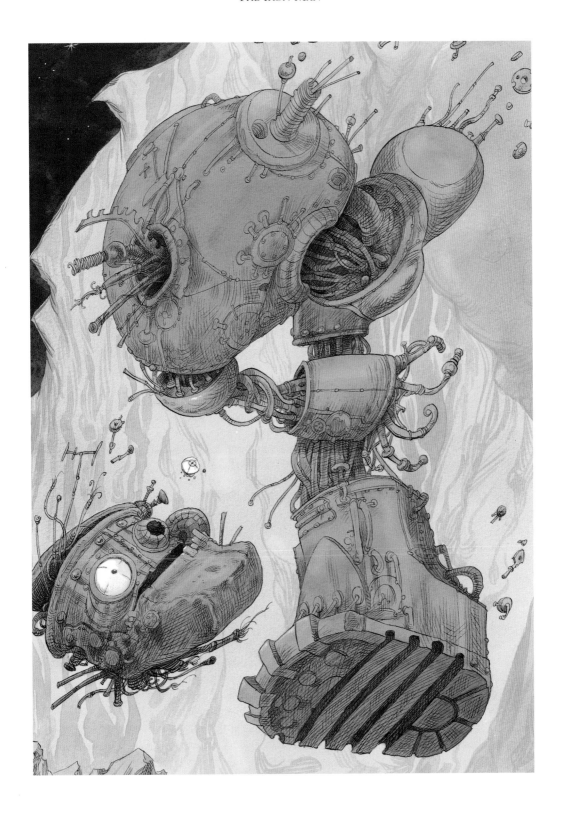

Something shiny, round and hard. It was one of the Iron Man's eyes. He brought it back to his mate. They both looked at this strange thing. And the eye looked at them. It rolled from side to side looking first at one gull, then at the other. The gulls, peering at it, thought it was a strange kind of clam, peeping at them from its shell.

Then the other gull flew up, wheeled around and landed and picked something up. Some awkward, heavy thing. The gull flew low and slowly, dragging the heavy thing. Finally, the gull dropped it beside the eye. This new thing had five legs. It moved. The gulls thought it was a strange kind of crab. They thought they had found a strange crab and a strange clam. They did not know they had found the Iron Man's eye and the Iron Man's right hand.

But as soon as the eye and the hand got together the eye looked at the hand. Its light glowed blue. The hand stood up on three fingers and its thumb, and craned its forefinger like a long nose. It felt around. It touched the eye. Gleefully it picked up the eye, and tucked it under its middle finger. The eye peered out, between the forefinger and thumb. Now the hand could see.

It looked around. Then it darted and jabbed one of the gulls with its stiffly held finger, then darted at the other and jabbed him. The two gulls flew up into the wind with a frightened cry.

Slowly then the hand crept over the stones, searching. It ran forward suddenly, grabbed something and tugged. But the thing was stuck between two rocks. The thing was one of the Iron Man's arms. At last the hand left the arm and went scuttling hither and thither among the rocks, till it stopped, and touched something gently. This thing was the other hand. This new hand stood up and hooked its finger round the little finger of the hand with the eye, and let itself be led. Now the two hands, the seeing one leading the blind one, walking on their fingertips, went back together to the arm, and together they tugged it free. The hand with the eye fastened itself on to the wrist of the arm. The arm stood up and walked on its hand. The other hand clung on behind as before, and this strange trio went searching.

An eye! There it was, blinking at them speechlessly beside a black and white pebble. The seeing hand fitted the eye to the blind hand and now both hands could see. They went running among the rocks. Soon they found a leg. They jumped on top of the leg and the leg went hopping over the rocks with the arm swinging from the hand that clung to the top of the leg. The other hand clung on top of that hand. The two hands, with their eyes, guided the leg, twisting it this way and that, as a rider guides a horse.

Soon they found another leg and the other arm. Now each hand, with an eye under its palm and an arm dangling from its wrist, rode on a leg separately about the beach. Hop, hop, hop, they went, peering among the rocks. One found an ear and at the same moment the other found the giant torso. Then the busy hands fitted the legs to the torso, then they fitted the arms, each fitting the other, and the torso stood up with legs and arms but no head. It walked about the beach, holding its eyes up in its hands, searching for its lost head. At last, there was the head eyeless, earless, nested in a heap of red seaweed. Now in no time the Iron Man had fitted his head back, and his eyes were in place, and everything in place except for one ear. He strode about the beach searching for his lost ear, as the sun rose over the sea and the day came.

The two gulls sat on their ledge, high

on the cliff. They watched the immense man striding to and fro over the rocks below. Between them, on the nesting ledge, lay a great iron ear. The gulls could not eat it. The baby gulls could not eat it. There it lay on the high ledge.

Far below, the Iron Man searched.

At last he stopped, and looked at the sea. Was he thinking the sea had stolen his ear? Perhaps he was thinking the sea had come up, while he lay scattered, and had gone down again with his ear.

He walked towards the sea. He walked into the breakers, and there he stood for a while, the breakers bursting around his knees. Then he walked in deeper, deeper, deeper.

The gulls took off and glided down low over the great iron head that was now moving slowly out through the swell. The eyes blazed red, level with the wavetops, till a big wave covered them and foam spouted over the top of the head. The head still moved out under water. The eyes and the top of the head appeared for a moment in a hollow of the swell. Now the eyes were green. Then the sea covered them and the head.

The gulls circled low over the line of bubbles that went on moving slowly out into the deep sea.

RUSSELL HOBAN

FROM *The Mouse and His Child*

ILLUSTRATED BY JUSTIN TODD

The sky was beginning to pale, and the air was sharp with morning as Ralphie and the mouse and his child came through the woods along a path to the Meadow Mutual Hoard and Trust Company, an earthen bank beside a stream. There were many tracks in the snow, and following these, they went through the entrance between the roots of a great sycamore tree.

The interior of the bank was chill and dim and hushed; the acorn-cup tallow lamps did little more than cast their own shadows and catch the glint of frost and mica on the earth walls. In the half-light a drowsy chipmunk teller looked up from the sunflower seeds he was counting as the rat walked in with the mouse and his child. The father pushed the son up to the rock behind which the chipmunk sat, then stood treading the ground until his spring unwound. The chipmunk looked at the paper bag they carried, then at Ralphie, and he felt for the alarm twig with his foot.

'Um yes,' he said. 'May I help you?'

Ralphie squinted cautiously into the shadows around him, saw no guards, and at once forgot everything Manny Rat had told him. 'All right,' he said, snarling and showing his teeth, 'this is a stick-up. Take me to the vault.'

'Um yes, sir!' said the chipmunk, stepping hard on the alarm twig as he spoke. The twig passed through a hole in the dirt wall behind him, and its other end vibrated against the snout of the badger guard who was dozing behind the stone that was the door of the vault. The badger woke up and smiled.

'This way, please,' said the chipmunk. Ralphie wound up the mouse father, and they went through a short tunnel to where the stone blocked the opening of the vault. 'Here is the vault,' said the chipmunk.

'Well, open it up,' said Ralphie.

'Um certainly,' said the chipmunk. He moved the stone and stepped out of the way as Ralphie rushed into the waiting jaws of the badger, who ate him up.

'Them city fellows ain't much at robbing banks,' chuckled the badger when he had finished, 'but they're good eating. Young fellows nowadays, they don't know how to pull a job. All they know is hurry, hurry, hurry.' He picked his teeth with a sliver of bone. 'What about them other two?' he asked the chipmunk.

The chipmunk looked back through the tunnel and out past the entrance of the bank. The mouse and his child, spun about by the violence of Ralphie's rush into the vault, had stumbled out of the Meadow Mutual Hoard and Trust company into the blue dawn, leaving their paper bag behind them. The chipmunk watched them walk down the path until they bumped into a rock and fell over. He shook his head. 'Whatever they are, they're harmless,' he said. 'Let them go.'

The mouse and his child lay in the snow where they had fallen, rattling with tinny, squeaking laughter. 'Skreep, skreep, skreep!' laughed the father. 'The frog was right – Ralphie did go on a long journey.'

'Skreek, skreek!' laughed the child. 'There was good eating too, for the badger! Skreek!'

'Seven o'clock!' called the clock on the steeple of the church across the meadow as it struck the hour.

'Listen!' said the father as he heard it. 'It's time for silence. Skreep!' And he began laughing all over again.

'If it's time for silence, how is it that we're still talking, Papa?' giggled the child.

'You've already broken one of the clockwork rules by crying on the job,' said the father, 'so we might as well break the other one too, and have done with it.'

'But I've often tried to speak after dawn,' said the child, 'and I never could till now. I wonder how it happened?'

'Perhaps your laughter freed you from the ancient clockwork laws,' said a deep voice, and the bullfrog fortune-teller hopped out from behind a tree. In the daylight he seemed smaller than he had at night, and much of his mystery was gone. He was not a young frog; the glove

he wore was shabby. In the cold light of morning he could be clearly seen for what he was: an old, eccentric traveller, neither respectable nor reliable, hung with odd parcels, tricked out with a swinging coin, and plying his trade where chance might take him. He set the mouse and his child on their feet and considered them thoughtfully. 'I have never heard a toy laugh before,' he said.

'Did you see what happened?' said the father, and he told the frog about the attempted bank robbery.

'A rash youth, Ralphie,' said Frog. 'He had no patience, poor boy! For once I read the future truly, and it came with fearful swiftness. But are you not curious about my presence here?'

'Why are you here?' asked the child.

'Because I followed you,' said Frog. 'Something draws me to you, and in the seeds I saw your fate and mine bound inextricably together. I said nothing at the time – I was afraid. There were dark and fearful things in that design, and unknown perils that can only be revealed by time.' He shook his head, and the coin swung like a pendulum from the string around his neck.

'Are you still afraid?' asked the father.

'Utterly,' said Frog. 'Do you choose to go ahead?'

'There is no going back,' said the father; 'we cannot dance in circles any more. Will you be our friend, and travel with us?'

'Be my uncle,' said the child. 'Be my Uncle Frog.'

'Ah!' said Frog. 'I had better make no promises; I am at best an infirm vessel. Do not expect too much. I will be your friend and uncle for as long as our destined roads may lie together; more than that I cannot say.' He gestured towards the snowy meadow that sparkled in the sunlight beyond the trees ahead, and pointed back along the shadowy pathway they had taken to the bank. 'Which shall it be?' he said. 'Towards the town, or out into the open country?'

'Maybe we could look for the elephant and the seal and the doll's house that used to be in the store with us,' said the child. 'Couldn't we, Papa?'

'What in the world for?' said the father.

'So we can have a family and be cosy,' answered the child.

'To begin with,' said the father, 'I cannot imagine myself being cosy with that elephant. But, putting that aside for the moment, the whole idea of such a quest is impossible. Despite what she said, she and the doll's house were very likely for sale just as we and the seal were, and by now they might be anywhere at all. It would be hopeless to attempt to find any of them.'

'She sang me a lullaby,' said the child.

'Really,' said the father, 'this is absurd.'

'I want the elephant to be my mama and I want the seal to be my sister and I want to live in the beautiful house,' the child insisted.

'What is all this talk of elephants and seals?' asked Frog.

'It's nonsense,' said the father, 'and yet it's not the child's fault. Our motor is in me. He fills the empty space inside himself with foolish dreams that cannot possibly come true.'

'Not so very foolish, perhaps,' said Frog. 'This seal, was she made of tin, and black and shiny? Did she have a small platform on her nose that revolved while a sparrow performed acrobatic tricks on it?'

'No,' said the father. 'She had a red and yellow ball on her nose.'

'She could have lost the ball,' said the

child. 'Maybe she does have a platform on her nose now. Where is the seal you saw?' he asked Frog.

'I don't know where she is now,' said Frog. 'But two years ago she was with a travelling theatrical troupe that comes to the pine woods every year.'

'If Uncle Frog could take us there, maybe we could find the seal,' said the mouse child to his father, 'and then we could all look for the elephant together.'

'Finding the elephant would be as pointless as looking for her,' said the father. 'But since I cannot convince you of that, we might just as well travel to the pine woods as anywhere else. At any rate we shall see something of the world.'

'Very well,' said Frog. 'On to the pine woods.'

'EXTRA!' screamed a raucous voice above them as a bluejay flashed by in the sunlight. 'RAT SLAIN IN BANK HOLD-UP ATTEMPT. WIND-UPS FLEE WITH GETAWAY FROG. LATE SCORES: WOODMICE LEAD MEADOW TEAM IN ACORN BOWLING. VOLES IDLE.'

ROALD DAHL

FROM *Charlie and the Chocolate Factory*

ILLUSTRATED BY QUENTIN BLAKE

During the next two weeks, the weather turned very cold. First came the snow. It began very suddenly one morning just as Charlie Bucket was getting dressed for school. Standing by the window, he saw the huge flakes drifting slowly down out of an icy sky that was the colour of steel.

By evening, it lay four feet deep around the tiny house, and Mr Bucket had to dig a path from the front door to the road.

After the snow, there came a freezing gale that blew for days and days without stopping. And oh, how bitter cold it was! Everything that Charlie touched seemed to be made of ice, and each time he stepped outside the door, the wind was like a knife on his cheek.

Inside the house little jets of freezing air came rushing in through the sides of the windows and under the doors, and there was no place to go to escape them. The four old ones lay silent and huddled in their bed, trying to keep the cold out of their bones. The excitement over the Golden Tickets had long since been forgotten. Nobody in the family gave a thought now to anything except the two vital problems of trying to keep warm and trying to get enough to eat.

There is something about very cold weather that gives one an enormous appetite. Most of us find ourselves beginning to crave rich steaming stews and hot apple pies and all kinds of delicious warming dishes; and because we are all a great deal luckier than we realize, we usually get what we want – or near enough. But Charlie Bucket never got what he wanted because the family couldn't afford it, and as the cold weather went on and on, he became ravenously and desperately hungry. Both bars of chocolate, the birthday one and the one Grandpa Joe had bought, had long since been nibbled away, and all he got now were those thin, cabbagy meals three times a day.

Then all at once, the meals became even thinner.

The reason for this was that the toothpaste factory, the place where Mr Bucket worked, suddenly went bust and had to close down. Quickly, Mr Bucket tried to get another job. But he had no luck. In the end, the only way in which he managed to earn a few pennies was by shovelling snow in the streets. But it wasn't enough to buy even a quarter of the food that seven people needed. The situation became desperate. Breakfast was a single slice of bread for each person now, and lunch was maybe half a boiled potato.

Slowly but surely, everybody in the house began to starve.

And every day, little Charlie Bucket, trudging through the snow on his way to school, would have to pass Mr Willy Wonka's giant chocolate factory. And every day, as he came near to it, he would lift his small pointed nose high in the air and sniff the wonderful sweet smell of melting chocolate. Sometimes, he would stand motionless outside the gates for several minutes on end, taking deep swallowing breaths as though he were trying to *eat* the smell itself.

'That child,' said Grandpa Joe, poking his head up from under the blanket one icy morning, 'that child has *got* to have more food. It doesn't matter about us. We're too old to bother with. But a *growing boy*! He can't go on like this! He's beginning to look like a skeleton!'

'What can one *do?*' murmured Grandma Josephine miserably. 'He refuses to take any of ours. I hear his mother tried to slip her own piece of bread on to his plate at breakfast this morning, but he wouldn't

touch it. He made her take it back.'

'He's a fine little fellow,' said Grandpa George. 'He deserves better than this.'

The cruel weather went on and on.

And every day, Charlie Bucket grew thinner and thinner. His face became frighteningly white and pinched. The skin was drawn so tightly over the cheeks that you could see the shapes of the bones underneath. It seemed doubtful whether he could go on much longer like this without becoming dangerously ill.

And now, very calmly, with that curious wisdom that seems to come so often to small children in times of hardship, he began to make little changes here and there in some of the things that he did, so as to save his strength. In the mornings, he left the house ten minutes earlier so that he could walk slowly to school, without ever having to run. He sat quietly in the classroom during break, resting himself, while the others rushed outdoors and threw snowballs and wrestled in the snow. Everything he did now, he did slowly and carefully, to prevent exhaustion.

Then one afternoon, walking back home with the icy wind in his face (and incidentally feeling hungrier than he had ever felt before), his eye was caught suddenly by something silvery lying in the gutter, in the snow. Charlie stepped off the kerb and bent down to examine it. Part of it was buried under the snow, but he saw at once what it was . . .

It was a half-crown piece!

Quickly he looked around him.

Had somebody just dropped it?

No – that was impossible because of the way part of it was buried.

Several people went hurrying past him on the pavement, their chins sunk deep in the collars of their coats, their feet crunching in the snow. None of them was searching for any money; none of them was taking

the slightest notice of the small boy crouching in the gutter.

Then was it *his,* this half-crown?

Could he *have* it?

Carefully, Charlie pulled it out from under the snow. It was damp and dirty, but otherwise perfect.

A WHOLE half-crown!

He held it tightly between his shivering fingers, gazing down at it. It meant one thing to him at that moment, only *one* thing. It meant FOOD.

Automatically, Charlie turned and began moving towards the nearest shop. It was only ten paces away . . . it was a newspaper and stationery

shop, the kind that sells almost everything, including sweets and cigars
. . . and what he would *do,* he whispered quickly to himself . . . he would
buy one luscious bar of chocolate and eat it *all* up, every bit of it, right
then and there . . . and the rest of the money he would take straight
back home and give to his mother.

Charlie entered the shop and laid the damp half-crown on the
counter.

'One Wonka's Whipple-Scrumptious Fudgemallow Delight,' he said,
remembering how much he had loved the one he had on his birthday.

The man behind the counter looked fat and well fed. He had big lips
and fat cheeks and a very fat neck. The fat around his neck bulged out
all around the top of his collar like a rubber ring. He turned and
reached behind him for the chocolate bar, then he turned back again
and handed it to Charlie. Charlie grabbed it and quickly tore off the
wrapper and took an enormous bite. Then he took another . . . and
another . . . and oh, the joy of being able to cram large pieces of
something sweet and solid into one's mouth! The sheer blissful joy of
being able to fill one's mouth with rich solid food!

'You look like you wanted that one, sonny,' the shopkeeper said pleasantly.

Charlie nodded, his mouth bulging with chocolate.

The shopkeeper put Charlie's change on the counter. 'Take it easy,' he said. 'It'll give you a tummy-ache if you swallow it like that without chewing.'

Charlie went on wolfing the chocolate. He couldn't stop. And in less than half a minute, the whole thing had disappeared down his throat. He was quite out of breath, but he felt marvellously, extraordinarily happy. He reached out a hand to take the change. Then he paused. His eyes were just above the level of the counter. They were staring at the little silver coins lying there. The coins were all sixpences. There were four of them altogether. Surely it wouldn't matter if he spent just one more.

'I think,' he said quietly, 'I think . . . I'll have just one more of those chocolate bars. The same kind as before, please.'

'Why not?' the fat shopkeeper said, reaching behind him again and taking another Whipple-Scrumptious Fudgemallow Delight from the shelf. He laid it on the counter.

Charlie picked it up and tore off the wrapper . . . and *suddenly* . . . from underneath the wrapper . . . there came a brilliant flash of gold.

Charlie's heart stood still.

'It's a Golden Ticket!' screamed the shopkeeper, leaping about a foot in the air. 'You've got a Golden Ticket! You've found the last Golden Ticket! Hey, would you believe it! Come and look at this, everybody! The kid's found Wonka's last Golden Ticket! There it is! It's right there in his hands!'

PHILIPPA PEARCE

FROM *Tom's Midnight Garden*

ILLUSTRATED BY GREG BECKER

That evening Tom went to bed as usual, and kept deliberate watch. His uncle and aunt seemed so slow in going to bed and to sleep! Twice Tom dozed, woke with a start, and went to his bedroom door and looked out; and there was still a light from under the door of the other bedroom. The third time, it had gone; and, after the shortest wait that prudence required, Tom crept out and downstairs as before, to the hall. As he went along it, the grandfather clock began striking for what must be midnight.

'I hope the moon's well up, outside,' Tom thought. 'I shall need light for getting across the yard. It would be awkward to make a noise out there – falling over dustbins or the car or anything.'

The grandfather clock had reached the thirteenth stroke as he slid his fingers up the edge of the door to find the knob of the Yale lock. He could not find it. He felt again. There was no Yale lock.

He did not understand; but he tried the bolt. It had been shot home; that was how the door was fastened now. Now he knew – he knew! With trembling fingers he began to ease the bolt back into a well-oiled, rustless socket.

The grandfather clock was striking on and on. Upstairs Alan Kitson, wakened by it, humped his shoulders fretfully: 'It's midnight. What on earth does the clock think it's striking?'

His wife did not answer.

'Striking hours and hours that don't exist! I only hope it's keeping Mrs Bartholomew awake, too!'

But Alan Kitson would have been disappointed if he had seen Mrs Bartholomew. She was lying tranquilly in bed: her false teeth, in a glass of water by the bedside, grinned unpleasantly in the moonlight, but her indrawn mouth was curved in a smile of easy, sweet-dreaming sleep. She was dreaming of the scenes of her childhood.

And the grandfather clock still went on striking, as if it had lost all count of time; and, while it struck, Tom, with joy in his heart, drew the bolt, turned the door-handle, opened the door and walked out into his garden, that he knew was waiting for him.

There is a time, between night and day, when landscapes sleep. Only the earliest riser sees that hour; or the all-night traveller, letting up the

blind of his railway-carriage window, will look out on a rushing landscape of stillness, in which trees and bushes and plants stand immobile and breathless in sleep – wrapped in sleep, as the traveller himself wrapped his body in his great-coat or his rug the night before.

This grey, still hour before morning was the time in which Tom walked into his garden. He had come down the stairs and along the hall to the garden door at midnight; but when he opened that door and stepped out into the garden, the time was much later. All night – moonlit or swathed in darkness – the garden had stayed awake; now, after that night-long vigil, it had dozed off.

The green of the garden was greyed over with dew; indeed, all its colours were gone until the touch of sunrise. The air was still, and the tree-shapes crouched down upon themselves. One bird spoke; and there was a movement when an awkward parcel of feathers dislodged itself from the tall fir-tree at the corner of the lawn, seemed for a second to fall and then at once swept up and along, outspread, on a wind that never blew, to another, farther tree: an owl. It wore the ruffled, dazed appearance of one who has been up all night.

Tom began to walk round the garden, on tiptoe. At first he took the outermost paths, gravelled and box-edged, intending to map for himself their farthest extent. Then he broke away impatiently on a cross-path. It tunnelled through the gloom of yew-trees arching overhead from one side, and hazel nut stubs from the other: ahead was a grey-green triangle of light where the path must come out into the open again. Underfoot the earth was soft with the humus of last year's rotted leaves. As he slipped along, like a ghost, Tom noticed, through gaps in the yew-trees on his right, the flick of a lighter colour than the yew: dark – light – dark – light – dark . . . The lighter colour, he realized, was the back of the house that he was glimpsing, and he must be passing behind the line of yew-trees that faced it across the lawn.

His path came out by the asparagus beds of the kitchen-garden – so he found them later to be. Beyond their long, grave-like mounds was a dark oblong – a pond. At one end of the pond, and overlooking it, stood an octagonal summer-house with an arcaded base and stone steps up to its door. The summer-house, like the rest of the garden, was asleep on its feet.

Beyond the pond and the summer-house was another path, meandering in idle curves. On the other side of this path was a stretch of wilderness, and then a hedge.

Of the four sides of the garden, Tom had already observed that three were walled: one by the back of the house itself, another by a very high south wall, built of clunch blocks and brick; and another by a lower wall that might well prove climbable. A hedge, however, is almost always more easily passed than any wall; and Tom had no sooner got into his garden than he was curious to see outside it. Sharp-eyed, he searched the hedge for a way through: he only needed such a little hole for a push and a wriggle. Here was a narrow gap, at last; but, to his surprise, it led into the hedge instead of directly through it. From this entry a passage – about a foot wide and three feet high – had been worn along in the heart of the hedge. Tom crept along it.

The tunnel came to an end where there was another, bolder gap into the open, this time out on to the far side of the hedge. Tom found himself looking out over a meadow. There were cows in the meadow: some still at their night's rest; one getting up, hindlegs first; and one already at the day's work of eating. This last cow stopped grazing to stare at Tom, as though she

thought she must still be dreaming. Stalks of grass hung from the sides of her mouth, and a long trickle of saliva descended from her lip and swung slightly in the little morning breeze that was getting up.

At the far side of the meadow a long, grey goose-neck rose from among the grasses, and Tom could see the bird's head turn sideways so that an eye could fix itself upon the gap in the hedge and the movement there. As a matter of fact, the look-out was a gander, although Tom did not know it; a moment later, the white necks of his wives rose round him, watching too. Then the gander strained his neck and breast upwards, and stretched his wings out into a splendid double curve – every pinion apart – and clapped them to and fro. First one goose and then another did the same, saluting the new morning.

Tom, made uneasily aware of the passage of time, crept back by the way he had come – back into the garden. He began to make himself familiar with it – its paths and alleys and archways, its bushes and trees. He noted some of its landmarks. At a corner of the lawn, a fir-tree towered up above all the other trees of the garden; it was wound about with ivy, through which its boughs stuck out like a child's arms through the wrappings of a shawl. On the high south wall, half covered by the sporting of a vine, there was a sundial; it was surmounted by a stone sun with stone rays, and its chin was buried in curly stone clouds – looking like his father's chin covered with shaving lather, Tom thought. To one side of the sundial, under a honeysuckle archway, was a door: Tom might have tried it, but the sight of the sundial, even without the sun upon it yet, had reminded him again of the passing of time. He hurried.

At the greenhouse, he did no more than look through the glass at the plants inside, and at the water tank, where a gleam came and went – perhaps a goldfish waking. The raised cucumber-frames by the greenhouse were walked round in less than a minute. He passed hastily along beside the aviary, where fan-tail pigeons were beginning to pick

their way across the brick floor.

He criss-crossed the kitchen-garden beyond the asparagus beds: fruit trees and strawberry beds and bean poles and a chicken-wire enclosure where raspberry canes and gooseberry bushes and currant bushes lived sheltered from the attack of birds. Beside the gooseberry wire grew a row of rhubarb. Each clump was covered with the end of an old tub or pot drain-pipe with sacking over the top. Between the loose staves of one of the tub-ends was something white – a piece of paper. It was folded, and addressed in a childish hand – if one could call it an address: 'To Oberon, King of Fairies.' Tom certainly did not want to be mixed up with talk of fairies and that kind of thing; and he moved very quickly away from the rhubarb bed.

He came out upon the lawn again. Here were the flower-beds – the crescent-shaped corner-beds with the hyacinths, among which an early bee was already working. The hyacinths reminded Tom of his Aunt

Gwen, but no longer with resentment. She knew nothing – poor thing! – and could be blamed for nothing, after all.

At the verge of the lawn, Tom stopped abruptly. On the grey-green of the dewed grass were two clearly defined patches of darker green: footprints. Feet had walked on to the lawn and stood there; then they had turned back and walked off again. How long ago? Surely since Tom had entered the garden. 'I'm sure they weren't here when I came out. Certain.'

How long had whoever it was stood there, and why? He or she had faced the line of yew-trees opposite; and that thought made Tom uneasy. When he had passed behind those trees and seen the flick-flick-flick of the house between them, had someone stood on the lawn watching the flick-flick-flick of Tom as he went?

Tom looked at the house, letting his eye go from window to window. Had someone drawn out of sight at an upper window? No, no: now he was just imagining things.

E. B. WHITE

FROM *Charlotte's Web*

ILLUSTRATED BY GARTH WILLIAMS

One evening, a few days after the writing had appeared in Charlotte's web, the spider called a meeting of all the animals in the barn cellar.

'I shall begin by calling the roll. Wilbur?'

'Here!' said the pig.

'Gander?'

'Here, here, here!' said the gander.

'You sound like three ganders,' muttered Charlotte. 'Why can't you just say "here"? Why do you have to repeat everything?'

'It's my idio-idio-idiosyncrasy,' replied the gander.

'Goose?' said Charlotte.

'Here, here, here!' said the goose. Charlotte glared at her.

'Goslings, one through seven?'

'Bee-bee-bee!' 'Bee-bee-bee!' 'Bee-bee-bee!' 'Bee-bee-bee!' 'Bee-bee-bee!' 'Bee-bee-bee!' 'Bee-bee-bee!' said the goslings.

'This is getting to be quite a meeting,' said Charlotte. 'Anybody would think we had three ganders, three geese, and twenty-one goslings. Sheep?'

'He-aa-aa!' answered the sheep all together.

'Lambs?'

'He-aa-aa!' answered the lambs all together.

'Templeton?'

No answer.

'Templeton?'

No answer.

'Well, we are all here except the rat,' said Charlotte. 'I guess we can

proceed without him. Now, all of you must have noticed what's been going on around here the last few days. The message I wrote in my web, praising Wilbur, has been received. The Zuckermans have fallen for it, and so has everybody else. Zuckerman thinks Wilbur is an unusual pig, and therefore he won't want to kill him and eat him. I dare say my trick will work and Wilbur's life can be saved.'

'Hurray!' cried everybody.

'Thank you very much,' said Charlotte. 'Now I called this meeting in order to get suggestions. I need new ideas for the web. People are already getting sick of reading the words "SOME PIG!" If anybody can think of another message, or remark, I'll be glad to weave it into the web. Any suggestions for a new slogan?'

'How about "Pig Supreme"?' asked one of the lambs.

'No good,' said Charlotte. 'It sounds like a rich dessert.'

'How about "Terrific, terrific, terrific"?' asked the goose.

'Cut that down to one "terrific" and it will do very nicely,' said Charlotte. 'I think "terrific" might impress Zuckerman.'

'But Charlotte,' said Wilbur, 'I'm not terrific.'

'That doesn't make a particle of difference,' replied Charlotte. 'Not a particle. People believe almost anything they see in print. Does anybody here know how to spell "terrific"?'

'I think,' said the gander, 'it's tee double ee double rr double rr double eye double ff double eye double see see see see see.'

'What kind of acrobat do you think I am?' said Charlotte in disgust. 'I would have to have St Vitus's Dance to weave a word like that into my web.'

'Sorry, sorry, sorry,' said the gander.

Then the oldest sheep spoke up. 'I agree that there should be something new written in the web if Wilbur's life is to be saved. And if Charlotte needs help in finding words, I think she can get it from our friend Templeton. The rat visits the dump regularly and has access to old magazines. He can tear out bits of advertisements and bring them up here to the barn cellar, so that Charlotte can have something to copy.'

'Good idea,' said Charlotte. 'But I'm not sure Templeton will be willing to help. You know how he is – always looking out for himself, never thinking of the other fellow.'

'I bet I can get him to help,' said the old sheep. 'I'll appeal to his baser instincts, of which he has plenty. Here he comes now. Everybody keep quiet while I put the matter up to him!'

The rat entered the barn the way he always did – creeping along close to the wall.

'What's up?' he asked, seeing the animals assembled.

'We're holding a directors' meeting,' replied the old sheep.

'Well, break it up!' said Templeton. 'Meetings bore me.' And the rat began to climb a rope that hung against the wall.

'Look,' said the old sheep, 'next time you go to the dump, Templeton, bring back a clipping from a magazine. Charlotte needs new ideas so she can write messages in her web and save Wilbur's life.'

'Let him die,' said the rat. 'I should worry.'

'You'll worry all right when next winter comes,' said the sheep. 'You'll worry all right on a zero morning next January when Wilbur is dead and nobody comes down here with a nice pail of warm slops to pour into the trough. Wilbur's left-over food is your chief source of supply, Templeton. *You* know that. Wilbur's food is your food; therefore Wilbur's destiny and your destiny are closely linked. If Wilbur is killed and his trough stands empty day after day, you'll grow so thin we can look right through your stomach and see objects on the other side.'

Templeton's whiskers quivered.

'Maybe you're right,' he said gruffly. 'I'm making a trip to the dump tomorrow afternoon. I'll bring back a magazine clipping if I can find one.'

'Thanks,' said Charlotte. 'The meeting is now adjourned. I have a busy evening ahead of me. I've got to tear my web apart and write TERRIFIC.'

Wilbur blushed. 'But I'm *not* terrific, Charlotte. I'm just about average for a pig.'

'You're terrific as far as *I'm* concerned,' replied Charlotte, sweetly, 'and that's what counts. You're my best friend, and *I* think you're sensational. Now stop arguing and go and get some sleep!'

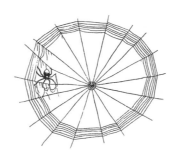

MARY NORTON

FROM *The Borrowers*

ILLUSTRATED BY PAUL BIRKBECK

Arrietty watched him move away from the step and then she looked about her. Oh, glory! Oh, joy! Oh, freedom! The sunlight, the grasses, the soft, moving air and halfway up the bank, where it curved round the corner, a flowering cherry-tree! Below it on the path lay a stain of pinkish petals and, at the tree's foot, pale as butter, a nest of primroses.

Arrietty threw a cautious glance towards the front doorstep and then, light and dancey, in her soft red shoes, she ran towards the petals. They were curved like shells and rocked as she touched them. She gathered several up and laid them one inside the other . . . up and up

. . . like a card castle. And then she spilled them. Pod came again to the top of the step and looked along the path. 'Don't you go far,' he said after a moment. Seeing his lips move, she smiled back at him: she was too far already to hear the words.

A greenish beetle, shining in the sunlight, came towards her across the stones. She laid her fingers

lightly on its shell and it stood still, waiting and watchful, and when she moved her hand the beetle went swiftly on. An ant came hurrying in a busy zigzag. She danced in front of it to tease it and put out her foot. It stared at her, nonplussed, waving its antennae; then pettishly, as though put out, it swerved away. Two birds came down, quarrelling shrilly, into the grass below the tree. One flew away but Arrietty could see the other among the moving grass stems above her on the slope. Cautiously she moved towards the bank and climbed a little nervously in amongst the green blades. As she parted them gently with her bare hands, drops of water plopped on her skirt as she felt the red shoes become damp. But on she went, pulling herself up now and again by rooty stems into this jungle of moss and wood-violet and creeping leaves of clover. The sharp-seeming grass blades, waist high, were tender to the touch and sprang back lightly behind her as she passed. When at last she reached the foot of the tree, the bird took fright and flew away and she sat down suddenly on a gnarled leaf of primrose. The air was filled with scent. 'But nothing will play with you,' she thought and saw the cracks and furrows on the primrose leaves held crystal beads of dew. If she pressed the leaf these rolled like marbles. The bank was warm, almost too warm here within the shelter of the tall grass, and the sandy earth smelled dry. Standing up, she picked a primrose. The pink stalk felt tender and living in her hands and was covered with silvery hairs, and when she held the flower, like a parasol, between her eyes and the sky, she saw the sun's pale light through the veined petals. On a piece of bark she found a wood-louse and she struck it lightly with her swaying flower. It curled immediately and became a ball, bumping softly away downhill in amongst the grass roots. But she knew about wood-lice. There were plenty of them at home under the floor. Homily always scolded her if she played with them because, she said, they smelled of old knives. She lay back among the stalks of the primroses and they made a coolness between her and the sun, and then, sighing,

she turned her head and looked sideways up the bank among the grass stems. Startled, she caught her breath. Something had moved above her on the bank. Something had glittered. Arrietty stared.

It was an eye. Or it looked like an eye. Clear and bright like the colour of the sky. An eye like her own but enormous. A glaring eye. Breathless with fear, she sat up. And the eye blinked. A great fringe of lashes came curving down and flew up again out of sight. Cautiously, Arrietty moved her legs: she would slide noiselessly in among the grass stems and slither away down the bank.

101

'Don't move!' said a voice, and the voice, like the eye, was enormous but, somehow, hushed – and hoarse like a surge of wind through the grating on a stormy night in March.

Arrietty froze. 'So this is it,' she thought, 'the worst and most terrible thing of all: I have been "seen"! Whatever happened to Eggletina will now, almost certainly, happen to me!'

There was a pause and Arrietty, her heart pounding in her ears, heard the breath again drawn swiftly into the vast lungs. 'Or,' said the voice, whispering still, 'I shall hit you with my ash stick.'

Suddenly Arrietty became calm. 'Why?' she asked. How strange her own voice sounded! Crystal thin and harebell clear, it tinkled on the air.

'In case,' came the surprised whisper at last, 'you ran towards me, quickly, through the grass . . . in case,' it went on, trembling a little, 'you scrabbled at me with your nasty little hands.'

Arrietty stared at the eye; she held herself quite still. 'Why?' she asked again, and again the word tinkled – icy cold it sounded this time, and needle sharp.

'Things do,' said the voice. 'I've seen them. In India.'

Arrietty thought of her

Gazetteer of the World. 'You're not in India now,' she pointed out.

'Did you come out of the house?'

'Yes,' said Arrietty.

'From whereabouts in the house?'

Arrietty stared at the eye. 'I'm not going to tell you,' she said at last bravely.

'Then I'll hit you with my ash stick!'

'All right,' said Arrietty, 'hit me!'

'I'll pick you up and break you in half!'

Arrietty stood up. 'All right,' she said and took two paces forward.

There was a sharp gasp and an earthquake in the grass: he spun away from her and sat up, a great mountain in a green jersey. He had fair, straight hair and golden eyelashes. 'Stay where you are!' he cried.

Arrietty stared up at him. So this was 'the boy'! Breathless, she felt, and light with fear. 'I guessed you were about nine,' she gasped after a moment.

He flushed. 'Well, you're wrong, I'm ten.' He looked down at her, breathing deeply. 'How old are you?'

'Fourteen,' said Arrietty. 'Next June,' she added, watching him.

There was silence while Arrietty waited, trembling a little. 'Can you read?' the boy said at last.

'Of course,' said Arrietty. 'Can't you?'

'No,' he stammered. 'I mean – yes. I mean I've just come from India.'

'What's that got to do with it?' said Arrietty.

'Well, if you're born in India, you're bilingual. And if you're bilingual, you can't read. Not so well.'

Arrietty stared up at him: what a monster, she thought, dark against the sky.

'Do you grow out of it?' she asked.

He moved a little and she felt the cold flick of his shadow.

'Oh yes,' he said, 'it wears off. My sisters were bilingual; now they

aren't a bit. They could read any of those books upstairs in the
schoolroom.'

'So could I,' said Arrietty quickly, 'if someone could hold them, and
turn the pages. I'm not a bit bilingual. I can read anything.'

'Could you read out loud?'

'Of course,' said Arrietty.

'Would you wait here while I run upstairs and get a book now?'

'Well,' said Arrietty; she was longing to show off; then a startled look
came into her eyes. 'Oh –', she faltered.

'What's the matter?' The boy was standing up now. He towered
above her.

'How many doors are there in this house?' She squinted up at him
against the bright sunlight. He dropped on one knee.

'Doors?' he said. 'Outside doors?'

'Yes.'

'Well, there's the front door, the back door, the gun-room door, the kitchen door, the scullery door . . . and the french windows in the drawing room.

'Well, you see,' said Arrietty, 'my father's in the hall, by the front door, working. He . . . he wouldn't want to be disturbed.'

'Working?' said the boy. 'What at?'

'Getting material,' said Arrietty, 'for a scrubbing-brush.'

'Then I'll go in the side door.' He began to move away but turned suddenly and came back to her. He stood a moment, as though embarrassed, and then he said: 'Can you fly?'

'No,' said Arrietty, surprised; 'can you?'

His face became even redder. 'Of course not,' he said angrily; 'I'm not a fairy!'

'Well, nor am I,' said Arrietty, 'nor is anybody. I don't believe in them.'

He looked at her strangely. 'You don't believe in them?'

'No,' said Arrietty; 'do you?'

'Of course not!'

Really, she thought, he is a very angry kind of boy.

'My mother believes in them,' she said, trying to appease him. 'She thinks she saw one once. It was when she was a girl and lived with her parents behind the sand pile in the potting-shed.'

He squatted down on his heels and she felt his breath on her face: 'What was it like?' he asked.

'About the size of a glow-worm with wings like a butterfly. And it had a tiny little face, she said, all alight and moving like sparks and tiny moving hands. Its face was changing all the time, she said, smiling and sort of shimmering. It seemed to be talking, she said, very quickly – but you couldn't hear a word . . .'

'Oh,' said the boy, interested. After a moment he asked: 'Where did it go?'

'It just went,' said Arrietty. 'When my mother saw it, it seemed to be caught in a cobweb. It was dark at the time. About five o'clock on a winter's evening. After tea.'

'Oh,' he said again and picked up two petals of cherry-blossom which he folded like a sandwich and ate slowly. 'Supposing,' he said, staring past her at the wall of the house, 'you saw a little man, about as tall as a pencil, with a blue patch in his trousers, half-way up a window curtain, carrying a doll's tea-cup – would you say it was a fairy?'

'No,' said Arrietty, 'I'd say it was my father.'

'Oh,' said the boy, thinking this out, 'does your father have a blue patch on his trousers?'

'Not on his best trousers. He does on his borrowing ones.'

'Oh,' said the boy again. He seemed to find it a safe sound, as lawyers do. 'Are there many people like you?'

'No,' said Arrietty. 'None. We're all different.'

'I mean as small as you?'

Arrietty laughed. 'Oh, don't be silly!' she said. 'Surely you don't think there are many people in the world your size?'

C. S. Lewis

FROM *The Lion, the Witch and the Wardrobe*

ILLUSTRATED BY GREG BECKER

'But what are you?' said the Queen again. 'Are you a great overgrown dwarf that has cut off his beard?'

'No, your Majesty,' said Edmund, 'I never had a beard, I'm a boy.'

'A boy!' said she. 'Do you mean you are a Son of Adam?'

Edmund stood still, saying nothing. He was too confused by this time to understand what the question meant.

'I see you are an idiot, whatever else you may be,' said the Queen. 'Answer me, once and for all, or I shall lose my patience. Are you human?'

'Yes, your Majesty,' said Edmund.

'And how, pray, did you come to enter my dominions?'

'Please, your Majesty, I came in through a wardrobe.'

'A wardrobe? What do you mean?'

'I − I opened a door and just found myself here, your Majesty,' said Edmund.

'Ha!' said the Queen, speaking more to herself than to him. 'A door. A door from the world of men! I have heard of such things. This may wreck all. But he is only one, and he is easily dealt with.' As she spoke these words she rose from her seat and looked Edmund full in the face, her eyes flaming; at the same moment she raised her wand. Edmund felt sure that she was going to do something dreadful but he seemed unable to move. Then, just as he gave himself up for lost, she appeared to change her mind.

'My poor child,' she said in quite a different voice, 'how cold you look! Come and sit with me here on the sledge and I will put my mantle round you and we will talk.'

Edmund did not like this arrangement at all but he dared not disobey; he stepped on to the sledge and sat at her feet, and she put a fold of her fur mantle round him and tucked it well in.

'Perhaps something hot to drink?' said the Queen. 'Should you like that?'

'Yes please, your Majesty,' said Edmund, whose teeth were chattering.

The Queen took from somewhere among her wrappings a very small bottle which looked as if it were made of copper. Then, holding out her arm, she let one drop fall from it on the snow beside the sledge. Edmund saw the drop for a second in mid-air, shining like a diamond. But the moment it touched the snow there was a hissing sound and there stood a jewelled cup full of something that steamed. The dwarf immediately took this and handed it to Edmund with a bow and a smile; not a very nice smile. Edmund felt much better as he began to sip the hot drink. It was something he had never tasted before, very sweet and foamy and creamy, and it warmed him right down to his toes.

'It is dull, Son of Adam, to drink without eating,' said the Queen presently. 'What would you like best to eat?'

'Turkish Delight, please, your Majesty,' said Edmund.

The Queen let another drop fall from her bottle on to the snow, and instantly there appeared a round box, tied with green silk ribbon, which, when opened, turned out to contain several pounds of the best Turkish Delight. Each piece was sweet and light to the very centre and Edmund had never tasted anything more delicious. He was quite warm now, and very comfortable.

While he was eating the Queen kept asking him questions. At first Edmund tried to remember that it is rude to speak with one's mouth full, but soon he forgot about this and thought only of trying to shovel down as much Turkish Delight as he could, and the more he ate the more he wanted to eat, and he never asked himself why the Queen should be so inquisitive. She got him to tell her that he had one brother and two sisters, and that one of his sisters had already been in Narnia and had met a Faun there, and that no one except himself and his brother and his sisters knew anything about Narnia. She seemed especially interested in the fact that there were four of them, and kept on coming back to it. 'You are sure there are just four of you?' she asked. 'Two Sons of Adam and two Daughters of Eve, neither more nor less?' and Edmund, with his mouth full of Turkish Delight, kept on saying, 'Yes, I told you that before,' and forgetting to call her 'Your Majesty', but she didn't seem to mind now.

At last the Turkish Delight was all finished and Edmund was looking very hard at the empty box and wishing that she would ask him whether he would like some more. Probably the Queen knew quite well what he was thinking; for she knew, though Edmund did not, that this was enchanted Turkish Delight and that anyone who had once tasted it would want more and more of it, and would even, if they were allowed, go on eating it till they killed themselves. But she did not offer him any more. Instead, she said to him,

'Son of Adam, I should so much like to see your brother and your two sisters. Will you bring them to see me?'

'I'll try,' said Edmund, still looking at the empty box.

'Because, if you did come again – bringing them with you of course – I'd be able to give you some more Turkish Delight. I can't do it now, the magic will only work once. In my own house it would be another matter.'

'Why can't we go to your house now?' said Edmund. When he had first got on to the sledge he had been afraid that she might drive away with him to some unknown place from which he would not be able to get back; but he had forgotten about that fear now.

'It is a lovely place, my house,' said the Queen. 'I am sure you would like it. There are whole rooms full of Turkish Delight, and what's more, I have no children of my own. I want a nice boy whom I could bring up as a Prince and who would be King of Narnia when I am gone. While he was Prince he would wear a gold crown and eat Turkish Delight all day long; and you are much the cleverest and handsomest young man I've ever met, I think I would like to make you the Prince – some day, when you bring the others to visit me.'

'Why not now?' said Edmund. His face had become very red and his mouth and fingers were sticky. He did not look either clever or handsome, whatever the Queen might say.

'Oh, but if I took you there now,' said she, 'I shouldn't see your brother and your sisters. I very much want to know your charming relations. You are to be the Prince and – later on – the King; that is

111

understood. But you must have courtiers and nobles. I will make your brother a Duke and your sisters Duchesses.'

'There's nothing special about *them*,' said Edmund, 'and, anyway, I could always bring them some other time.'

'Ah, but once you were in my house,' said the Queen, 'you might forget all about them. You would be enjoying yourself so much that you wouldn't want the bother of going to fetch them. No. You must go back to your own country now and come to me another day, *with them,* you understand. It is no good coming without them.'

'But I don't even know the way back to my own country,' pleaded Edmund.

'That's easy,' answered the Queen. 'Do you see that lamp?' She pointed with her wand and Edmund turned and saw the same lamp-post under which Lucy had met the Faun. 'Straight on, beyond that, is the way to the World of Men. And now look the other way' – here she pointed in the opposite direction – 'and tell me if you can see two little hills rising above the trees.'

'I think I can,' said Edmund.

'Well, my house is between those two hills. So next time you come you have only to find the lamp-post and look for those two hills and walk through the wood till you reach my house. But remember – you must bring the others with you. I might have to be very angry with you if you came alone.'

'I'll do my best,' said Edmund.

'And, by the way,' said the Queen, 'you needn't tell them about me. It would be fun to keep it a secret between us two, wouldn't it? Make it a surprise for them. Just bring them along to the two hills – a clever boy like you will easily think of some excuse for doing that – and when you come to my house you could just say "Let's see who lives here" or something like that. I am sure that would be best. If your sister has met one of the Fauns, she may have heard strange stories about me – nasty stories that might make her afraid to come to me. Fauns will say anything, you know, and now –'

'Please, please,' said Edmund suddenly, 'please couldn't I have just one piece of Turkish Delight to eat on the way home?'

'No, no,' said the Queen with a laugh, 'you must wait till next time.' While she spoke, she signalled to the dwarf to drive on, but as the sledge swept away out of sight, the Queen waved to Edmund, calling out, 'Next time! Next time! Don't forget. Come soon.'

Edmund was still staring after the sledge when he heard someone calling his own name, and looking round he saw Lucy coming towards him from another part of the wood.

'Oh, Edmund!' she cried. 'So you've got in too! Isn't it wonderful and now –'

'All right,' said Edmund, 'I see you were right and it is a magic wardrobe after all. I'll say I'm

sorry if you like. But where on earth have you been all this time? I've been looking for you everywhere.'

'If I'd known you had got in I'd have waited for you,' said Lucy, who was too happy and excited to notice how snappishly Edmund spoke or how flushed and strange his face was. 'I've been having lunch with dear Mr Tumnus, the Faun, and he's very well and the White Witch has done nothing to him for letting me go, so he thinks she can't have found out and perhaps everything is going to be all right after all.'

'The White Witch?' said Edmund; 'who's she?'

'She is a perfectly terrible person,' said Lucy. 'She calls herself the Queen of Narnia though she has no right to be queen at all, and all the Fauns and Dryads and Naiads and Dwarfs and Animals – at least all the good ones – simply hate her. And she can turn people into stone and do all kinds of horrible things. And she has made a magic so that it is always winter in Narnia – always winter, but it never gets to Christmas. And she drives about on a sledge, drawn by reindeer, with her wand in her hand and a crown on her head.'

Edmund was already feeling uncomfortable from having eaten too many sweets, and when he heard that the Lady he had made friends with was a dangerous witch he felt even more uncomfortable. But he still wanted to taste that Turkish Delight again more than he wanted anything else.

'Who told you all that stuff about the White Witch?' he asked.

'Mr Tumnus, the Faun,' said Lucy.

'You can't always believe what Fauns say,' said Edmund, trying to sound as if he knew far more about them than Lucy.

'Who said so?' asked Lucy.

'Everyone knows it,' said Edmund; 'ask anybody you like. But it's pretty poor sport standing here in the snow. Let's go home.'

'Yes, let's,' said Lucy. 'Oh, Edmund, I *am* glad you've got in too. The others will have to believe in Narnia now that both of us have been there. What fun it will be!'

But Edmund secretly thought that it would not be as good fun for him as for her. He would have to admit that Lucy had been right, before all the others, and he felt sure the others would all be on the side of the Fauns and the animals; but he was already more than half on the side of the Witch. He did not know what he would say, or how he would keep his secret once they were all talking about Narnia.

By this time they had walked a good way. Then suddenly they felt coats around them instead of branches and next moment they

were both standing outside the wardrobe in the empty room.

'I say,' said Lucy, 'you do look awful, Edmund. Don't you feel well?'

'I'm all right,' said Edmund, but this was not true. He was feeling very sick.

'Come on then,' said Lucy, 'let's find the others. What a lot we shall have to tell them! And what wonderful adventures we shall have now that we're all in it together.'

B. B.

FROM *The Little Grey Men*

ILLUSTRATED BY JUSTIN TODD

When the gnomes awakened on the following evening they found a change in the weather. They had slept during the day in a willow root close to a deep brown pool, bored out by the floods of many winters. Hunger demanded immediate appeasement, and they began at once to put their fishing lines together.

Gone was the golden weather which had so far favoured their trip; instead the sky was overcast and gloomy, and a strong wind was whipping the trees and bushes, turning the pale undersides of the leaves uppermost. Curious swirls and V-shaped eddy-marks creased the pool by the willow; the reeds bent and bent again before the rude breath of the stormy wind, their sharp tips cutting the water.

On all sides stretched the lush meadows; the gnomes could see the waves of wind passing over the moving grass so that the surface was undulating exactly like the surface of the sea, the rollers following one behind another, a sea of grass instead of water. Though the evening was not cold, the gnomes were glad of their skin coats.

In a very short time they had caught some thumping perch, and they fished until they had broken all their hooks. They were not used to these heavy game fish. Seven fat fellows lay on the root of the willow when they at last wound in their lines, and you may depend upon it, it was not long before those fish were neatly cut up and grilled over a fire. They ate themselves cross-eyed and for some time were quite incapable of movement.

'It's almost like an autumn night,' remarked Baldmoney at length, as he lit his pipe with an ember from the fire; 'we're going to have rain before dawn, that's why the fish are biting.'

Sneezewort was homesick and also very full of perch, so he did not answer. He watched the wind ripples passing over the moving grass and the spots of yellow foam spinning slowly round the pool; a little higher upstream there was a big clot of it caught against a submerged reed.

He was thinking how cosy the oak root would be on a night like this, and how the glow of the fire used to light up the rugged interior of the tree. How was the owl family getting on, and Dodder, and Watervole? Perhaps after all they had made a mistake to come on this trip; a lot might have happened to Cloudberry in all those months which had passed since he went away. And truth to say, there was something a little sinister in this gloomy evening, and the chasing ripples and sighing wind seemed heavy with foreboding.

The next instant his heart gave a bump, and all these sentimental thoughts had gone in the instinct of self-preservation. For downstream, threading its way close to the water, was the lithe brown form of one of their most dreaded enemies, Stoat! He was puzzling on their scent. Unknown to them he had followed them for a long way along the Folly bank; now the scent was getting stale and he was almost on the point of giving up.

With a lightning-like movement both gnomes were on their feet, for both had seen their dreaded enemy almost at the same instant. There

was no chance of climbing up inside the willow, for the barrel of the tree was not hollow. They must make a break for it while there was time. To be cornered inside the root would be disastrous.

Each had the presence of mind to grab his stick and bundle. They slipped out of the tree, keeping it between them and their pursuer, and made their way as fast as they could up the stream. Not far distant it took a wide bend to the left and the bank was clothed with thick bushes, but stoats can climb bushes with agility.

Their safest chance lay in a tree up which they could climb. Unfortunately, as you may have noticed, few trees have branches very low to the ground which would have given them a start, and, anyway, there was not a tree in sight save some elms across the meadow. The gnomes might have made a dash for these, but if the stoat was really hot on their trail, he could overtake them. When in a hurry the little

devil in brown can move like lightning.

One point was in their favour, they had a good start, and stoats do not as a rule hunt by sight until they are very near their quarry.

The gnomes ran as fast as they could up the shingle; now and again they glanced over their shoulders. Stoat had gone inside the willow stump and was smelling around. Perhaps he would find the heads and bones of the perch which might delay him, but it was a forlorn hope. Such things happened at the Oak Pool, but they were never far from the old tree, and when chased could simply run inside and bar the door.

For the next ten minutes they ran as fast as their short legs could carry them. Baldmoney led, but after a while began to get a little puffed. Sneezewort, in better training and lighter build, began to make the running.

They reached the bend and the next moment their pursuer was hidden from view; perhaps he would give up the chase and content himself with exploring the willow root. Both gnomes were now puffing and blowing; their little anxious faces, always red at the best of times, were deep crimson and beads of sweat rolled off them. The heavy bundles hampered them in their flight, but they contained all they possessed and would not be abandoned unless things became very hot indeed.

'I can't see him,' gasped Sneezewort, looking back.

'Don't stop running,' puffed Baldmoney, 'he's very likely still on our trail.'

Round the bend there was a fallen log which lay almost across the stream. The water gurgled and swilled round the end of it, deep and swift, but it was jumpable. They scurried across the log and landed safely on the far bank, though Baldmoney, tired and spent, wet his right leg to the knee. They found themselves in a dense sedge-bed. The ground was miry and black, but they plunged in among the reeds.

A startled water-vole plopped into the stream and a reed-bunting flew up, excitedly flirting his white-edged tail and looking about on all sides at the shaking reeds.

Had you or I been standing on the bank we should have thought a rat or mouse was rustling through the water plants, for the gnomes were quite hidden, only the sedges quivered. At last, the reeds thinned and in their place a forest of sturdy dock plants, with stout and hairy stems, raised their broad umbrellas overhead. It was fine cover, but no cover in the world avails a gnome or rabbit when a stoat is once on the hunting trail, so they pushed on.

Then the docks thinned and they could see the light once more and the brown Folly open to the sky, crinkling in a thousand catspaws over a wide shallow, and beyond, a deep pool. They crossed the shallows to their original bank hoping that the stoat would lose the scent in the running water. They were now utterly spent and must find some sort of hiding-place. Leaning over the pool was a willow branch, its main stem half awash, and the slender rods grew straight up in a thick pallisade. Right at the end the gnomes caught sight of a moorhen's nest; it might have been one of the many 'rest' nests that the cock bird builds as rafts for his babies when they are hatched. You will nearly always find two moorhens' nests belonging to the same pair of birds.

They would have liked to have gone farther, but both were blown, and this was the only possible cover in sight. They crept out along the half-submerged branch, squeezing in between the willow wands until they reached the nest, and into it they tumbled, one on top of the other.

The nest, which contained three handsome eggs (quite cold, for the hen had not begun to sit), was substantially built, but very damp. They made themselves as small as possible, squeezing in between the eggs and taking care not to break them, and lay peeping fearfully down the stream.

Below them the brown water slid and hissed, strings of bubbles showed far down under the surface and the gnomes could see shoals of little silver minnows, a whole school of them, passing like a cloud.

'Is he following us?' whispered Baldmoney when he had got his breath. 'I can't see a sign of anything.'

Sneezewort did not reply. He was breathing so fast and his heart was a-hammering so quickly he could hardly see.

Downstream they could just discern the log where they had crossed to the far bank; beyond that, the bend and the steep sandy bank hid everything. There was nothing to be seen save an old rook flying across the rim of the meadow. He came oaring his way along and alighted on the shingle at the shallows where, after a quick look round on all sides, he began to hunt for mussels. Rooks and crows love freshwater mussels.

He waddled about in the shallow water and along the edge of the reed bed, turning over some old empty shells which he found lying about.

A large spot of rain came plop! into the pool, then another and another. They rattled on the leaves like bullets, the falling drops making little tents in the water. As the minutes passed the heavy breathing of the gnomes quietened and they began to feel secure. The rain, lashed by the wind, increased in violence and the gnomes began to shiver.

Up by the reed bed the rook had at last found a mussel and he flew away with it over the fields. The vista downstream showed no sign of life.

'I think he's given up,' whispered Baldmoney; 'he hasn't come any farther than the willow.'

Sneezewort, knowing the ways of stoats, was not so sure. It all depended whether the stoat was hungry.

As the gnomes lay in the bottom of the nest with their chins on the rim of it, it occurred to them what a fine meal the eggs would make. A big black water-boatman came up from the depths of the pool and lay on the surface with his oars outspread. And close to the nest a whole crowd of tiny silver beetles were weaving about on the surface of the water; they moved and glistened like minute racing cars.

Then the gnomes saw Stoat. He was puzzling up the bank, quartering the ground like a hound. He went along the log and stopped, for it was a big jump for him, and he did not like the look of it. At other times it might have been interesting to watch the little hunter at work, but it was no fun when the quarry was yourself, and Baldmoney and Sneezewort trembled with apprehension. Stoat ran back along the log and began coming up the bank on the other side. Then the gnomes realized that they had made a mistake – that they should not have recrossed the brook. Had they remained in the reed bed they would have been safe. But Stoat now had nothing to guide him. He came along slowly with frequent pauses, showing his yellowish-white chest as he sat up in the grass. When he ran, his body was arched in a hump, the black-tipped tail held high. Nearer and nearer he came, and the poor little gnomes crouched lower in the nest.

Stoat was now not more than thirty paces from their tree, and the next moment was at the shallows where they had crossed. He must have struck their scent then, for he came on at the hunting run with his muzzle fairly low.

Neither gnome spoke, but each loosened his knife in its leather sheath in a meaning sort of way, as though he meant to sell his life dearly.

Stoat reached the log; the watching gnomes could now see every detail of the cruel flat head, the sharp muzzle and the primrose-yellow chest. They could see the whiskers, like needles, and the working nose. He reared himself up on his hind legs with his front paws on the end of the willow branch, and the next moment was looking in their direction with cruel little button eyes. Then he began to come along the tree, threading the willow wands with lithe purpose.

Baldmoney and Sneezewort waited until he was almost at the nest before acting. Perhaps they were hypnotized by the deadly little beast. Had they been rabbits they would have simply sat back and squealed. But not so the gnomes. As Stoat came almost within springing distance they dived over the edge of the nest like young moorhens, one on one side, and one on the other, down into the brown water, taking their bundles with them.

Stoat chittered with rage, displaying a sudden

125

row of ivory needles. A foot away was the unhappy Sneezewort's head, drifting downstream with the current, and a little to the left, Baldmoney's, both swimming as gracefully as frogs.

For a second Stoat was inclined to follow, for stoats swim with ease. And then he saw the three smooth eggs lying in the cup of the nest. In a moment the gnomes were forgotten, here was a far greater delicacy, EGGS!

Stoats love a nice fresh egg; every year thousands of birds lose their precious clutches to the little brown robber. He climbs the blackthorn to get to the nest of blackbird and thrush, finch and blackcap, and not only eggs fall to him but baby birds as well.

In a second or two he was breaking open the moorhen's eggs, greedily sucking the contents, and then, when he had eaten them all, he curled round in the nest and went fast asleep like a full-fed dog.

J. R. R. Tolkien

From *The Hobbit*

ILLUSTRATED BY CHRIS RIDDELL

There they all sat glum and wet and muttering, while Oin and Gloin went on trying to light the fire, and quarrelling about it. Bilbo was sadly reflecting that adventures are not all pony-rides in May-sunshine, when Balin, who was always their look-out man, said: 'There's a light over there!' There was a hill some way off with trees on it, pretty thick in parts. Out of the dark mass of the trees they could now see a light shining, a reddish comfortable-looking light, as it might be a fire or torches twinkling.

When they had looked at it for some while, they fell to arguing. Some said 'no' and some said 'yes'. Some said they could but go and see, and anything was better than little supper, less breakfast, and wet clothes all the night.

Others said: 'These parts are none too well known, and are too near the mountains. Travellers seldom come this way now. The old maps are no use: things have changed for the worse and the road is unguarded. They have seldom even heard of the king round here, and the less inquisitive you are as you go along, the less trouble you are likely to find.' Some said: 'After all there are fourteen of us.' Others said: 'Where has Gandalf got to?' This remark was repeated by everybody. Then the rain began to pour down worse than ever, and Oin and Gloin began to fight.

That settled it. 'After all we have got a burglar with us,' they said; and so they made off, leading their ponies (with all due and proper caution) in the direction of the light. They came to the hill and were soon in the wood. Up the hill they went; but there was no proper path to be seen, such as might lead to a house or a farm; and do what they could they made a deal of rustling and crackling and creaking (and a good deal of grumbling and dratting), as they went through the trees in the pitch dark.

Suddenly the red light shone out very bright through the tree-trunks not far ahead.

'Now it is the burglar's turn,' they said, meaning Bilbo. 'You must go on and find out all about that light, and what it is for, and if all is perfectly safe and canny,' said Thorin to the hobbit. 'Now scuttle off, and come back quick, if all is well. If not, come back if you can! If you can't, hoot twice like a barn-owl and once like a screech-owl, and we will do what we can.' Off Bilbo had to go, before he could explain that he could not hoot even once like any kind of owl any more than fly like a bat. But at any rate hobbits can move quietly in woods, absolutely quietly. They take a pride in it, and Bilbo had sniffed more than once at what he called 'all this dwarvish racket', as they went along, though I don't suppose you or I would have noticed anything at all on a windy night, not if the whole cavalcade had passed two feet off. As for Bilbo walking primly towards the red light, I don't suppose even a weasel would have stirred a whisker at it. So, naturally, he got right up to the fire – for fire it was – without disturbing anyone. And this is what he saw.

Three very large persons sitting round a very large fire of beech-logs. They were toasting mutton on long spits of wood, and licking the gravy off their fingers. There was a fine toothsome smell. Also there was a barrel of good drink at hand, and they were drinking out of jugs. But they were trolls. Obviously trolls. Even Bilbo, in spite of his sheltered life, could see that: from the great heavy faces of them, and their size, and the shape of their legs, not to mention their language, which was not drawing-room fashion at all, at all.

'Mutton yesterday, mutton today, and blimey, if it don't look like mutton again tomorrer,' said one of the trolls.

'Never a blinking bit of manflesh have we had for long enough,' said a second. 'What the 'ell William was a-thinkin' of to bring us into these parts at all, beats me – and the drink runnin' short, what's more,' he said jogging the elbow of William, who was taking a pull at his jug.

William choked. 'Shut yer mouth!' he said as soon as he could. 'Yer can't expect folk to stop here for ever just to be et by you and Bert. You've et a village and a half between yer, since we come down from the mountains. How much more d'yer want? And time's been up our way, when yer'd have said "thank yer Bill" for a nice bit o' fat valley mutton like what this is.' He took a big bite off a sheep's leg he was toasting, and wiped his lips on his sleeve.

Yes, I am afraid trolls do behave like that, even those with only one head each. After hearing all this Bilbo ought to have done something at once. Either he should have gone back quietly and warned his friends that there were three fair-sized trolls at hand in a nasty mood, quite likely to try toasted dwarf, or even pony, for a change; or else he should have done a bit of good quick burgling. A really first-class and legendary burglar would at this point have picked the trolls' pockets – it is nearly always worthwhile, if you can manage it – pinched the very mutton off the spits, purloined the beer, and walked off without their noticing him. Others more practical but with less professional pride would perhaps have stuck a dagger into each of them before they observed it. Then the night could have been spent cheerily.

Bilbo knew it. He had read of a good many things he had never seen

or done. He was very much alarmed, as well as disgusted; he wished himself a hundred miles away, and yet – and yet somehow he could not go straight back to Thorin and Company empty-handed. So he stood and hesitated in the shadows. Of the various burglarious proceedings he had heard of, picking the trolls' pockets seemed the least difficult, so at last he crept behind a tree just behind William.

Bert and Tom went off to the barrel. William was having another drink. Then Bilbo plucked up courage and put his little hand in William's enormous pocket. There was a purse in it, as big as a bag to Bilbo. 'Ha!' thought he warming to his new work as he lifted it carefully out, 'this is a beginning!'

It was! Trolls' purses are the mischief, and this was no exception. ''Ere, oo are you?' it squeaked, as it left the pocket; and William turned round at once and grabbed Bilbo by the neck, before he could duck behind the tree.

'Blimey, Bert, look what I've copped!' said William.

'What is it?' said the others coming up.

'Lumme, if I knows! What are yer?'

'Bilbo Baggins, a bur–a hobbit,' said poor Bilbo, shaking all over, and wondering how to make owl-noises before they throttled him.

'A burrahobbit?' said they a bit startled. Trolls are slow in the uptake, and mighty suspicious about anything new to them.

'What's a burrahobbit got to do with my pocket, anyways?' said William.

'And can ye cook 'em?' said Tom.

'Yer can try,' said Bert, picking up a skewer.

'He wouldn't make above a mouthful,' said William, who had already had a fine supper, 'not when he was skinned and boned.'

'P'raps there are more like him round about, and we might make a pie,' said Bert. 'Here you, are there any more of your sort a-sneakin' in these here woods, yer nasty little rabbit,' said he looking at the hobbit's furry feet; and he picked him up by the toes and shook him.

'Yes, lots,' said Bilbo, before he remembered not to give his friends away. 'No none at all, not one,' he said immediately afterwards.

'What d'yer mean?' said Bert, holding him right way up, by the hair this time.

'What I say,' said Bilbo gasping. 'And please don't cook me, kind sirs! I am a good cook myself, and cook better than I cook, if you see what I mean. I'll cook beautifully for you, a perfectly beautiful breakfast for you, if only you won't have me for supper.'

'Poor little blighter,' said William. He had already had as much supper as he could hold; also he had had lots of beer. 'Poor little blighter! Let him go!'

'Not till he says what he means by *lots* and *none at all*,' said Bert. 'I don't want to have me throat cut in me sleep! Hold his toes in the fire, till he talks!'

'I won't have it,' said William. 'I caught him anyway.'

'You're a fat fool, William,' said Bert, 'as I've said afore this evening.'

'And you're a lout!'

'And I won't take that from you, Bill Huggins,' says Bert, and puts his fist in William's eye.

Then there was a gorgeous row. Bilbo had just enough wits left, when Bert dropped him on the ground, to scramble out of the way of their feet, before they were fighting like dogs, and calling one another all sorts of perfectly true and applicable names in very loud voices. Soon they were locked in one another's arms, and rolling nearly into the fire kicking and thumping, while Tom whacked at them both with a branch to bring them to their senses and that of course only made them madder than ever.

That would have been the time for Bilbo to have left. But his poor little feet had been very squashed in Bert's big paw, and he had no breath in his body, and his head was going round; so there he lay for a while panting, just outside the circle of firelight.

Right in the middle of the fight up came Balin. The dwarves had heard noises from a distance, and after waiting for some time for Bilbo to come back, or to hoot like an owl, they started off one by one to creep towards the light as quietly as they could. No sooner did Tom see Balin come into the light than he gave an awful howl. Trolls simply detest the very sight of dwarves (uncooked). Bert and Bill stopped fighting immediately, and 'a sack, Tom, quick!' they said. Before Balin, who was wondering where in all this commotion Bilbo was, knew what was happening, a sack was over his head, and he was down.

'There's more to come yet,' said Tom, 'or I'm mighty mistook. Lots and none at all, it is,' said he. 'No burrahobbits, but lots of these here dwarves. That's about the shape of it!'

'I reckon you're right,' said Bert, 'and we'd best get out of the light.'

And so they did. With sacks in their hands, that they used for carrying off mutton and other plunder, they waited in the shadows. As each dwarf came up and looked at the fire, and the spilled jugs, and the gnawed mutton, in surprise, pop! went a nasty smelly sack over his head, and he was down. Soon Dwalin lay by Balin, and Fili and Kili together, and Dori and Nori and Ori all in a heap, and Oin and Gloin and Bifur and Bofur and Bombur piled uncomfortably near the fire.

'That'll teach 'em,' said Tom; for Bifur and Bombur had given a lot of trouble, and fought like mad, as dwarves will when cornered.

Thorin came last – and he was not caught unawares. He came expecting mischief, and didn't need to see his friends' legs sticking out of sacks to tell him that things were not all well. He stood outside in the shadows some way off, and said: 'What's all this trouble? Who has been knocking my people about?'

'It's trolls!' said Bilbo from behind a tree. They had forgotten all about him. 'They're hiding in the bushes with sacks,' said he.

'Oh are they?' said Thorin, and he jumped forward to the fire, before they could leap on him. He caught up a big branch all on fire at one end; and Bert got that end in his eye before he could step aside. That put him out of the battle for a bit. Bilbo did his best. He caught hold of Tom's leg – as well as he could, it was thick as a young tree-trunk – but he was sent spinning up into the top of some bushes, when Tom kicked the sparks up in Thorin's face.

Tom got the branch in his teeth for that, and lost one of the front ones. It made him howl, I can tell you. But just at that moment William came up behind and popped a sack right over Thorin's head and down to his toes. And so the fight ended. A nice pickle they were all in now: all neatly tied up in sacks, with three angry trolls (and two with burns and bashes to remember) sitting by them, arguing whether they should roast them slowly, or mince them fine and boil them, or just sit on them one by one and squash them into jelly; and Bilbo up in a bush, with his clothes and his skin torn, not daring to move for fear they should hear him.

It was just then that Gandalf came back. But no one saw him. The trolls had just decided to roast the dwarves now and eat them later – that was Bert's idea, and after a lot of argument they had all agreed to it.

'No good roasting 'em now, it'd take all night,' said a voice. Bert thought it was William's.

'Don't start the argument all over again, Bill,' he said, 'or it *will* take all night.'

'Who's a-arguing?' said William, who thought it was Bert that had spoken.

'You are,' said Bert.

'You're a liar,' said William; and so the argument began all over again. In the end they decided to mince them fine and boil them. So they got a great black pot, and they took out their knives.

'No good boiling 'em! We ain't got no water, and it's a long way to the well and all,' said a voice. Bert and William thought it was Tom's.

'Shut up!' said they, 'or we'll never have done. And yer can fetch the water yerself, if ye say any more.'

'Shut up yerself!' said Tom, who thought it was William's voice. 'Who's arguing but you, I'd like to know.'

'You're a booby,' said William.

'Booby yerself!' said Tom.

And so the argument began all over again, and went on hotter than ever, until at last they decided to sit on the sacks one by one and squash them, and boil them next time.

'Who shall we sit on first?' said the voice.

'Better sit on the last fellow first,' said Bert, whose eye had been damaged by Thorin. He thought Tom was talking.

'Don't talk to yerself!' said Tom. 'But if you wants to sit on the last one, sit on him. Which is he?'

'The one with the yellow stockings,' said Bert.

'Nonsense, the one with the grey stockings,' said a voice like William's.

'I made sure it was yellow,' said Bert.

'Yellow it was,' said William.

'Then what did yer say

it was grey for?' said Bert.

'I never did. Tom said it.'

'That I never did!' said Tom. 'It was you.'

'Two to one, so shut yer mouth!' said Bert.

'Who are you a-talkin' to?' said William.

'Now stop it!' said Tom and Bert together. 'The night's gettin' on, and dawn comes early. Let's get on with it!'

'Dawn take you all, and be stone to you!' said a voice that sounded like William's. But it wasn't. For just at that moment the light came over the hill, and there was a mighty twitter in the branches. William never spoke for he stood turned to stone as he stooped; and Bert and Tom were stuck like rocks as they looked at him. And there they stand to this day, all alone, unless the birds perch on them; for trolls, as you probably know, must be underground before dawn, or they go back to the stuff of the mountains they are made of, and never move again. That is what had happened to Bert and Tom and William.

'Excellent!' said Gandalf, as he stepped from behind a tree, and helped Bilbo to climb down out of a thornbush. Then Bilbo understood. It was the wizard's voice that had kept the trolls bickering and quarrelling, until the light came and made an end of them.

NOEL STREATFEILD

FROM *Ballet Shoes*

ILLUSTRATED BY EMMA CHICHESTER CLARK

Petrova knew nothing of the technicalities of acting, and cared less; she just knew that 'timing' was saying a line at the right moment, instead of the wrong, and that 'pace' was picking up your cues properly, and she felt thankful that Mustard-seed said so little that once she had the 'And I' speech right, she could not go far wrong. She thought the rehearsals a frightful bore, but she brought her handbook on aeroplanes with her, and when not wanted for the fairy scenes, or to work at one of the innumerable ballets, would curl up in a corner, and study it.

One day they got a special call for five o'clock, and there they learnt a thing which pleased Pauline, and made Petrova take an entirely different view of rehearsals. They were to fly – Oberon, Titania, Puck, their four selves, and some extra fairies. The flying apparatus was on small trolleys in charge of men in the gallery from which the scenery was lowered. Petrova, who was ignorant of theatre terms, called them 'Men up in the roof', but Pauline said correctly that they were 'in the flies'.

Before flying they were fastened into small harnesses, to the back of which was fixed a wire. Petrova had hoped, when she heard that she was to fly, that she would be held up in the air by a wire, and could propel herself where she liked. It was not nearly as easy as that; but it was tremendous fun. Each actual flight that any of them made was done from a fixed point to a fixed point, which was managed by the angle of the wire to the trolley overhead. They could fly in any direction, because the trolley moved all round the flies; but they could not fly at all except on arranged cue to an arranged place.

Pauline, Petrova, and the extra fairies, trained as they were as dancers, in no time picked up the way to make a graceful flight; but the grown-ups had great difficulty. Oberon was a brilliant actor but a clumsy mover, and did not look a bit like a fairy king, but more like a sack of potatoes being lifted on a crane. Titania used her arms stiffly and awkwardly. Puck wanted to do strange Puck-like movements in the air, which were good ideas when they were in his head, but looked rather silly on the end of a wire. The whole flying rehearsal was more like a game than work, they laughed so much.

Petrova, with her birth certificate and two photographs, had, of course, been to the County Hall, to be examined for a licence. Pauline

came too, as the three months allowed on her last licence had long ago expired. Sylvia had a joint letter about their work from Doctor Jakes and Doctor Smith. This being Pauline's fourth licence, she and the County Council authorities were old friends. They knew this was the last licence she would need, and said they hoped she would go on with her savings-bank account. Petrova, though she was quite strong, did not look anything like as well as Pauline, as she was naturally thin and rather sallow. The doctor could find nothing wrong with her, though he took a long time examining her; but he told Sylvia she must be careful of her hours of rest, and horrified Petrova by suggesting extra milk. She had not Pauline's way of expecting everybody to be a friend, and was terrified by the London County Council man, and answered all his friendly questions with monosyllables, which made her sound bad-tempered, though she was not; only embarrassed at so much attention focussed on her.

'There,' said Pauline, when they got outside. 'I told you there was nothing to be frightened of. Aren't they nice?'

Petrova did not answer; she felt glad to have got her interview over, and her licence granted. She admitted in her mind that they were as nice as any people could be who had to examine you all over, and stare, and ask questions, but she was not feeling good-tempered enough to admit it.

There was a répétition générale of 'A

Midsummer Night's Dream' – at least, that was what the papers called it. Pauline and Petrova called it a dress rehearsal to which you could invite friends. The people invited by the management sat in the stalls, and friends of the principals in the dress circle, and the rest of the theatre was for those holding tickets from the ballet and walkers-on. Pauline and Petrova were each allowed to invite two friends. Nana would be behind with them, and Mr and Mrs Simpson were away, so they asked Sylvia, the two doctors, and Posy. Theo had a seat in any case, because quite a lot were sent to the Academy, as so many of the children were supplied from there. To begin with, Nana and Sylvia said that it was too late for Posy, and they could not think of allowing it; but Theo, hearing they were all going, and not the argument about Posy, managed to get seats in the pit for Cook and Clara. That settled it; Posy could not be left in the house alone, so she was allowed to come on the understanding that she went home when the others did, before the last act.

It was a lovely dress rehearsal. If there was any truth in the supposed superstition that a good dress rehearsal means a bad first performance, then the first night of 'A Midsummer Night's Dream' ought to have been the worst in history. Never was a production where so many things could have gone wrong. There were various traps and spring-boards for Puck, there were gauzes which hid Oberon, there was a most elaborate lighting plot, there were

difficult cues for the singers, done by lights because they were out of sight of the conductor's bâton, there was the flying – there were, in fact, dozens of things which might have gone wrong, quite apart from the usual drying-up due to nerves, and none of them did. From the first note of Mendelssohn's overture, to Puck's 'Give me your hands, if we be friends, And Robin shall restore amends,' the production was almost faultless, and quite exquisite. It had a real fairy quality, which not only the audience, but the actors, felt.

Pauline, flying over Bottom's head, with her silk wings streaming behind her, and her toe pointed to alight beside Titania, almost forgot to say 'ready' when she came down, because she was thinking to herself how like being a real fairy it was. Petrova, who made her first appearance peeping out from a tree, peered between the leaves at what was going on and thought it all very gay, and stopped wishing she was safely at home. In the dress circle, Doctor Smith and Doctor Jakes enjoyed themselves as true Shakespeareans always enjoy themselves, arguing between each act about the reading of the parts, and the way the lines were said. Fortunately they found plenty to disapprove of, or they would not have enjoyed themselves at all. Posy had never been to see a play before. In order that she should enjoy it, Doctor Jakes had taken great trouble to instruct her in the story; in spite of this, she found the lovers a bore, but was entranced by the rest of the play. She was most impressed by the work of the principal dancer, who, as she explained to Sylvia, was very good. Though forced to dance barefoot – a form of dancing for which she did not care so much as for work on the point – her elevation was quite remarkable.

'She should be good,' Sylvia pointed out. 'She has been principal ballerina in revues for quite a while.'

'I know.' Posy nodded. 'Madame told me. That's why I'm surprised she's good.'

'You are a snob, Posy,' Sylvia laughed. 'You've never seen a revue. How do you know what the standard of dancing is?'

Posy leant back in her seat.

'It's very low,' she said seriously. 'When we get home I'll show you: Madame has shown me.'

'When you get home you'll go to bed.' Sylvia looked down at Posy. 'I wish you wouldn't talk in that rather silly way. You are only ten; you can't know much about dancing, good or bad.'

'I do,' said Posy. 'I always shall.'

Sylvia gave up the argument.

'Well, come along; Nana will be waiting for you in the foyer; the other two must be changed by now.'

In the pit, Cook and Clara enjoyed themselves enormously.

'It's prettier than that "Blue Bird",' Cook sighed.

They nudged each other every time either Pauline or Petrova made an entrance. They were not much impressed by their clothes, though they had been well prepared for the worst by Nana. Petrova's hat was the thing that really worried them.

Cook gave Clara an expressive look.

'It's like the hat charabanc parties wear on outings.'

Clara made clicking noises with her tongue against her teeth.

'It's a shame, that's what it is. Petrova not having the looks that Pauline has, doesn't mean that they've got to make a comic of her.'

In the tube going home, Pauline and Petrova pestered Posy for criticism of the production; but the moment she made any, they sat on her, asking her what she thought she knew about it. Nana hurried them to bed when they got in, and told them not to talk. Pauline leaned over to Petrova's bed.

'Do you think you'll like working now you've started, Petrova?'

Petrova thought. She remembered what fun it was flying on a wire, and how much she, Pauline, and the other two fairies laughed in the dressing-room. Then she thought of her handbook on the mechanism of aeroplanes; as long as the play ran she would hardly have time to open it. She turned over in bed.

'Not very much, I don't think.'

Posy was considering the routine of the work of the première danseuse.

'You remember where it's getting dark and Derova comes through the trees and dances? I can remember it all but just the end, Pas Couru, Arabesque Developpé, then a Pas de Chat took her off; but there was one move in between. What was it?'

Pauline hummed the music.

'Balancé. Abaisser, then wasn't there a Jeté before the Pas de Chat?'

'You're both wrong.' Petrova sat up. 'It's not a Pas de Chat that takes her off, it's a Capriole; I noticed most particularly.'

Posy stood up on her bed.

'Really, Petrova Fossil. A Capriole! So.' She sprung on to her right foot, then jumped and beat her right calf neatly against her left. 'Did you see Derova do that beat? And if she didn't, then it wasn't a Capriole.'

'She goes off so quickly, you can't see what she does,' Petrova argued.

'I can. Pauline's right. Jeté.' Posy did it. 'Then Pas de Chat. So.' She gave another jump, this time with her right leg stretched to second position, then back with the knee bent, she finished almost off the bed with both knees bent, and her left leg across. 'Isn't that what she did, Pauline?'

'Almost.' Pauline got up. 'It's like this from after the grand Arabesque, Jeté, Glissé, Pas de Chat.'

She did it all beautifully, except that the end of her spring took her off the bed and on to the floor with a thump. She scrambled up to get back into bed; but before she was there, Nana opened the door, and turned on the lights. Nana looked at Pauline, and at the state her and Posy's beds were in, and she was really annoyed.

JOHN MASEFIELD

FROM A Box of Delights

ILLUSTRATED BY PAUL BIRKBECK

Now at last, Kay felt that he was free to look at the Box of Delights. He went up to his bedroom, but even there he was not sure that he could guard himself from being seen. Remembering how those spies had been peering in at the window the night before and how the repulsive Rat had crept about in the secret passages finding out all sorts of things, he locked both doors and hung caps over the keyholes, looked under the beds and finally, as in the past when he had wished to hide from his governess Sylvia Pouncer, he crept under the valance of his dressing-table. No one could possibly see him there.

The Box was of some very hard wood of a very dense grain, covered with shagreen which was black with age and sometimes worn away to show the wood beneath. Both wood and shagreen had been polished until they were as smooth as polished metal. On the side there was a little counter-sunk groove in the midst of which was a knob in the shape of a tiny golden rosebud.

Kay pressed the knob and at once from within the Box there came a crying of birds. As he listened he heard the stockdove brooding, the cuckoo tolling, blackbirds, thrushes and nightingales singing. Then a far-away cock crowed thrice and the Box slowly opened. Inside he saw what he took to be a book, the leaves of which were all chased and

worked with multitudinous figures, and the effect that it gave him was that of staring into an opening in a wood. It was lit from within and he saw that the tiny things that were shifting there were the petals of may-blossom from giant hawthorn trees covered with flowers. The hawthorns stood on each side of the entrance to the forest, which was dark from the great trees yet dappled with light. Now, as he looked into it, he saw deer glide with alert ears, then a fox, motionless at his earth, a rabbit moving to new pasture and nibbling at a dandelion and the snouts of the moles breaking the wet earth. All the forest was full of life, all the birds were singing, insects humming, dragonflies darting, butterflies wavering and settling. It was so clear that he could see the flies on the leaves brushing their heads and wings with their legs. 'It's all alive and it's full of summer, there are all the birds singing, there's a linnet, a bullfinch, a robin, and that's a little wren.' Others were singing too: different kinds of tits, the woodpecker drilling, the chiff-chaff repeating his name, the yellowhammer and garden-warbler, and overhead, as the bird went swiftly past, came the sad, laughing cry of the curlew. While he gazed into the heart of summer and listened to the murmur and the singing, he heard another noise like the tinkling of little bells.

'Where did I hear that noise before?' Kay said to himself. He remembered that strange rider who had passed him in the street the day before. That rider, who seemed to have little silver chains dangling from his wrists, had jingled so.

'Oh,' Kay said as he looked, 'there's someone wonderful coming.'

At first he thought the figure was one of those giant red deer, long since extinct, with enormous antlers. Then he saw that it was a great man, antlered at the brow, dressed in deerskin and moving with the silent, slow grace of a stag, yet hung about with little silver chains and bells.

Kay knew at once that this was Herne the Hunter, of whom he had often heard. 'Ha, Kay,' Herne said, 'are you coming into my wild wood?'

'Yes please, sir,' Kay said. Herne stretched out his hand, Kay took it and there he was in the forest between the two hawthorn trees, with the petals of the may-blossom falling on him. All the may-blossoms that fell were talking to him and he was aware of what all the creatures of the forest were saying to each other, what the birds were singing and what it was that the flowers and trees were thinking. And he realized that the forest went on and on for ever and all of it was full of life beyond anything that he had ever imagined, for in the trees, on each leaf and every twig and in every inch of soil there were ants, grubs, worms, little tiny, moving things, incredibly small and yet all thrilling with life.

'Oh dear,' Kay said, 'I shall never know a hundredth part of all the things there are to know.'

'You will, if you stay with me,' Herne the Hunter said. 'Would you like to be a stag with me in the wild wood?'

There was Kay in the green wood, beside a giant stag, so screened with the boughs that they were a part of a dappled pattern of light and shade and the news of the wood came to him in scents upon the wind. They moved off out of the green wood into a rolling grassland where some fox-cubs were playing with a vixen, and presently came down to a pool where moorhens were cocking about in the water, under the fierce eye of a crested grebe. It was lovely, Kay thought, to feel the water cool upon the feet after running, 'and it's lovely too,' he thought, 'to have hard feet and not get sharp bits of twigs into one's soles.' They moved through the water towards some reeds where Kay saw a multitude of wild duck.

'Would you like to be a wild duck, Kay?' Herne asked.

At once, with a great clatter of feathers, the wild duck rose more and more and more, going high up, and, oh joy! Herne and Kay were with them, flying on wings of their own and Kay could just see that his neck was glinting green. There was the pool, blue as a piece of sky below them and the sky above brighter than he had ever seen it. They flew higher and higher in great sweeps and presently they saw the sea like the dark blue on a map.

'Now for the plunge!' Herne cried and instantly they were surging down swiftly and still more swiftly and the pool was rushing up at them and they all went skimming into it with a long, scuttering, rippling splash. And there they all were, paddling together, happy to be in water again.

'How beautiful the water is,' Kay said. Indeed it was beautiful, clear hill-water, with little fish darting this way and that and the weeds waving.

'Would you like to be a fish, Kay?' Herne asked, and instantly Kay was a fish. He and Herne were there in the coolness and dimness, wavering as the water wavered and feeling a cold spring gurgling up just underneath them, tickling their tummies.

While Kay was enjoying the water Herne asked, 'Did you see the wolves in the wood?'

'No,' Kay said.

'Well, they were there,' Herne said, 'that was why I moved. Did you see the hawks in the air?'

'No,' Kay said.

'Well, they were there,' Herne said, 'and that was why I plunged. And do you see the pike in the weeds?'

'No,' Kay said.

'He is there,' Herne said. 'Look!'

Looking ahead up the stream Kay saw a darkness of weeds wavering in the water and presently a part of the darkness wavered into a shape with eyes that gleamed and hooky teeth that showed. Kay saw that the eyes were fixed upon himself and suddenly the dark shadow leaped swiftly forward with a swirl of water. But Kay and Herne were out of the water. They were trotting happily together over the grass towards the forest, Herne a giant figure with the antlers of the red stag and himself a little figure with budding antlers. And so they trotted together to a great ruined oak tree, so old that all within was hollow, though the great shell still put forth twigs and leaves.

Somehow the figure of Herne became like the oak tree and merged into it till Kay could see nothing but the tree. What had been Herne's antlers were now a few old branches and what had seemed silver chains dangling from Herne's wrists were now the leaves rustling. The oak tree faded and grew smaller till it was a dark point in a sunny glade, and there was Kay standing between the two hawthorn trees which were shedding their blossoms upon him. These too shrank until they were as tiny as the works of a watch and then Kay was himself again under the valance in his room at Seekings, looking at the first page in the Book of Delights contained within the Box.

'No wonder the old man called it a Box of Delights,' Kay said. 'Now I wonder how long I was in that fairyland with Herne the Hunter?' He looked at his watch and found that it was ten minutes to eleven. He had been away only two minutes.

RICHMAL CROMPTON

FROM *Just William*

ILLUSTRATED BY ROWAN CLIFFORD

I t all began with William's aunt, who was in a good temper that morning, and gave him a shilling for posting a letter for her and carrying her parcels from the grocer's.

'Buy some sweets or go to the Pictures,' she said carelessly, as she gave it to him.

William walked slowly down the road, gazing thoughtfully at the coin. After deep calculations, based on the fact that the shilling is the equivalent of two sixpences, he came to the conclusion that both luxuries could be indulged in.

In the matter of sweets, William frankly upheld the superiority of quantity over quality. Moreover, he knew every sweet shop within a two miles radius of his home whose proprietor added an extra sweet after the scale had descended, and he patronized these shops exclusively. With solemn face and eager eye, he always watched the process of weighing, and 'stingy' shops were known and banned by him.

He wandered now to his favourite confectioner and stood outside the window for five minutes, torn between the rival attractions of Gooseberry Eyes and Marble Balls. Both were sold at 4 ounces for 2d. William never purchased more expensive luxuries. At last his frowning brow relaxed and he entered the shop.

'Sixpennoth of Gooseberry Eyes,' he said, with a slightly self-conscious air. The extent of his purchases rarely exceeded a penny.

'Hello!' said the shopkeeper, in amused surprise.

'Gotter bit of money this mornin',' explained William carelessly, with the air of a Rothschild.

He watched the weighing of the emerald green dainties with silent intensity, saw with satisfaction the extra one added after the scale had fallen, received the precious paper bag, and, putting two sweets into his mouth, walked out of the shop.

Sucking slowly, he walked down the road towards the Picture Palace. William was not in the habit of frequenting Picture Palaces. He had only been there once before in his life.

It was a thrilling programme. First came the story of desperate crooks who, on coming out of any building, glanced cautiously up and down the street in huddled, crouching attitudes, then crept ostentatiously on their way in a manner guaranteed to attract attention and suspicion at any place and time. The plot was involved. They were pursued by police, they leapt on to a moving train and then, for no accountable reason, leapt from that on to a moving motor-car and from that they plunged into a moving river. It was thrilling and William thrilled. Sitting quite motionless, he watched, with wide, fascinated eyes, though his jaws never ceased their rotatory movement and every now and then his hand would go mechanically to the paper bag on his knees and convey a Gooseberry Eye to his mouth.

The next play was a simple country love-story, in which figured a simple country maiden wooed by the squire, who was marked out as the villain by his moustachios.

After many adventures the simple country maiden was won by a simple country son of the soil in picturesque rustic attire, whose emotions were faithfully portrayed by gestures that must have required much gymnastic skill; the villain was finally shown languishing in a prison cell, still indulging in frequent eye-brow play.

Next came another love-story – this time of a noblehearted couple, consumed with mutual passion and kept apart not only by a series of misunderstandings possible only in a picture play, but also by maidenly pride and reserve on the part of the heroine and manly pride and reserve on the part of the hero that forced them to hide their ardour beneath a cold and haughty exterior. The heroine's brother moved through the story like a good fairy, tender and protective towards his orphan sister and ultimately explained to each the burning passion of the other.

It was moving and touching and William was moved and touched.

The next was a comedy. It began by a solitary workman engaged upon the re-painting of a door and ended with a miscellaneous crowd of people, all covered with paint, falling downstairs on top of one another. It was amusing. William was riotously and loudly amused.

Lastly came the pathetic story of a drunkard's downward path. He began as a wild young man in evening clothes drinking intoxicants and playing cards, he ended as a wild old man in rags still drinking intoxicants and playing cards. He had a small child with a pious and superior expression, who spent her time weeping over him and exhorting him to a better life, till, in a moment of justifiable exasperation, he threw a beer bottle at her head. He then bedewed her bed in Hospital with penitent tears, tore out his hair, flung up his arms towards Heaven, beat his waistcoat, and clasped her to his breast, so that it was not to be wondered at that, after all that excitement, the child had a relapse and with the words 'Goodbye, Father. Do not think of what you have done. I forgive you' passed peacefully away.

William drew a deep breath at the end, and still sucking, arose with the throng and passed out.

Once outside, he glanced cautiously around and slunk down the road in the direction of his home. Then he doubled suddenly and ran down a back street to put his imaginary pursuers off his track. He took a pencil from his pocket and, levelling it at the empty air, fired twice. Two of his pursuers fell dead, the rest came on with redoubled vigour. There was no time to be lost. Running for dear life, he dashed down the next street, leaving in his wake an elderly gentleman nursing his toe and cursing volubly. As he neared his gate, William again drew the pencil from his pocket and, still looking back down the road, and firing as he went, he rushed into his own gateway.

William's father, who had stayed at home that day because of a bad headache and a touch of liver, picked himself up from the middle of a rhododendron bush and seized William by the back of his neck.

'You young ruffian,' he roared, 'what do you mean by charging into me like that?'

William gently disengaged himself.

'I wasn't chargin', Father,' he said, meekly. 'I was only jus' comin' in at the gate, same as other folks. I jus' wasn't looking jus' the way you were coming, but I can't look all ways at once, cause –'

'Be *quiet!*' roared William's father.

Like the rest of the family, he dreaded William's eloquence.

'What's that on your tongue? Put your tongue out.'

William obeyed. The colour of William's tongue would have put to shame Spring's freshest tints.

'How many times am I to tell you,' bellowed William's father, 'that I won't have you going about eating filthy poisons all day between meals?'

'It's not filthy poison,' said William. 'It's jus' a few sweets Aunt Susan gave me 'cause I kin'ly went to the post office for her an' –'

'Be quiet! Have you got any more of the foul things?'

'They're not foul things,' said William, doggedly. 'They're good. Jus' have one, an' try. They're jus' a few sweets Aunt Susan kin'ly gave me an' –'

'Be *quiet!* Where are they?'

Slowly and reluctantly William drew forth his bag. His father seized it and flung it far into the bushes. For the next ten minutes William conducted a thorough and systematic search among the bushes and for the rest of the day consumed Gooseberry Eyes and garden soil in fairly equal proportions.

KENNETH GRAHAME

FROM *The Wind in the Willows*

ILLUSTRATED BY JUSTIN TODD

During luncheon – which was excellent, of course, as everything at Toad Hall always was – the Toad simply let himself go. Disregarding the Rat, he proceeded to play upon the inexperienced Mole as on a harp. Naturally a voluble animal, and always mastered by his imagination, he painted the prospects of the trip and the joys of the open life and the road-side in such glowing colours that the Mole could hardly sit in his chair for excitement. Somehow, it soon seemed taken for granted by all three of them that the trip was a settled thing; and the Rat, though still unconvinced in his mind, allowed his good-nature to over-ride his personal objections. He could not bear to disappoint his two friends, who were already deep in schemes and anticipations, planning out each day's separate occupation for several weeks ahead.

When they were quite ready, the now triumphant Toad led his companions to the paddock and set them to capture the old grey horse, who, without having been consulted, and to his own extreme annoyance, had been told off by Toad for the dustiest job in this dusty expedition. He frankly preferred the paddock, and took a deal of catching. Meantime Toad packed the lockers still tighter with necessaries, and hung nose-bags, nets of onions, bundles of hay, and baskets from the bottom of the cart. At last the horse was caught and

harnessed, and they set off, all talking at once, each animal either trudging by the side of the cart or sitting on the shaft, as the humour took him. It was a golden afternoon. The smell of the dust they kicked up was rich and satisfying; out of thick orchards on either side of the road, birds called and whistled to them cheerily; good-natured wayfarers, passing them, gave them 'Good day', or stopped to say nice things about their beautiful cart; and rabbits, sitting at their front doors in the hedgerow, held up their fore-paws, and said, 'O my! O my! O my!'

Late in the evening, tired and happy and miles from home, they drew up on a remote common far from habitations, turned the horse loose to graze, and ate their simple supper sitting on the grass by the side of the cart. Toad talked big about all he was going to do in the days to come, while stars grew fuller and larger all around them, and a yellow moon, appearing suddenly and silently from nowhere in particular, came to keep them company and listen to their talk. At last they turned into their little bunks in the cart; and Toad, kicking out his legs, sleepily said, 'Well, good night, you fellows! This is the real life for a gentleman! Talk about your old river!'

'I *don't* talk about my river,' replied the patient Rat. 'You know I don't, Toad. But I *think* about it,' he added pathetically, in a lower tone: 'I think about it – all the time!'

The Mole reached out from under his blanket, felt for the Rat's paw in the darkness, and gave it a squeeze. 'I'll do whatever you like, Ratty,' he whispered. 'Shall we run away tomorrow morning, quite early – *very* early – and go back to our dear old hole on the river?'

'No, no, we'll see it out,' whispered back the Rat. 'Thanks awfully, but I ought to stick by Toad till this trip is ended. It wouldn't be safe for him to be left to himself. It won't take very long. His fads never do. Good night!'

The end was indeed nearer than even the Rat suspected.

After so much open air and excitement the Toad slept very soundly, and no amount of shaking could rouse him out of bed next morning. So the Mole and Rat turned to, quietly and manfully, and while the Rat saw to the horse, and lit a fire, and cleaned last night's cups and platters, and got things ready for breakfast, the Mole trudged off to the nearest village, a long way off, for milk and eggs and various necessaries the Toad had, of

course, forgotten to provide.
The hard work had all been
done, and the two animals
were resting, thoroughly
exhausted, by the time Toad
appeared on the scene, fresh
and gay, remarking what a
pleasant easy life it was they
were all leading now, after the
cares and worries and fatigues
of housekeeping at home.

They had a pleasant ramble
that day over grassy downs and along narrow by-lanes, and camped, as
before, on a common, only this time the two guests took care that Toad
should do his fair share of work. In consequence, when the time came
for starting next morning, Toad was by no means so rapturous about
the simplicity of the primitive life, and indeed attempted to resume his
place in his bunk, whence he was hauled by force. Their way lay, as
before, across country by narrow lanes, and it was not till the afternoon
that they came out on the high road, their first high road; and there
disaster, fleet and unforeseen, sprang out on them – disaster
momentous indeed to their expedition, but simply overwhelming in its
effect on the after-career of Toad.

They were strolling along the high road easily, the Mole by the
horse's head, talking to him, since the horse had complained that he
was being frightfully left out of it, and nobody considered him in the
least; the Toad and the Water Rat walking behind the cart talking
together – at least Toad was talking, and Rat was saying at intervals,
'Yes, precisely; and what did *you* say to *him*?' – and thinking all the time
of something very different, when far behind them they heard a faint
warning hum, like the drone of a distant bee. Glancing back, they saw

a small cloud of dust, with a dark centre of energy, advancing on them at incredible speed, while from out the dust a faint 'Poop-poop!' wailed like an uneasy animal in pain. Hardly regarding it, they turned to resume their conversation, when in an instant (as it seemed) the peaceful scene was changed, and with a blast of wind and a whirl of sound that made them jump for the nearest ditch, it was on them! The 'poop-poop' rang with a brazen shout in their ears, they had a moment's glimpse of an interior of glittering plate-glass and rich morocco, and the magnificent motor-car, immense, breath-snatching, passionate, with its pilot tense and hugging his wheel, possessed all earth and air for the fraction of a second, flung an enveloping cloud of dust that blinded and enwrapped them utterly, and then dwindled to a speck in the far distance, changed back into a droning bee once more.

The old grey horse, dreaming, as he plodded along, of his quiet paddock, in a new raw situation such as this simply abandoned himself to his natural emotions. Rearing, plunging, backing steadily, in spite of all the Mole's efforts at his head, and the Mole's lively language directed at his better feelings, he drove the cart backwards towards the deep ditch at the side of the road. It wavered an instant – then there was a heartrending crash – and the canary-coloured cart, their pride and their joy, lay on its side in the ditch, an irredeemable wreck.

The Rat danced up and down in the road, simply transported with passion. 'You villains!' he shouted, shaking both fists, 'you scoundrels, you highwaymen, you – you – road-hogs! – I'll have the law on you! I'll report you! I'll take you through all the Courts!' His homesickness had quite slipped away from him, and for the moment he was the skipper of the canary-coloured vessel driven on a shoal by the reckless jockeying of rival mariners, and he was trying to recollect all the fine and biting things he used to say to masters of steam-launches when their wash, as they drove too near the bank, used to flood his parlour carpet at home.

Toad sat straight down in the middle of the dusty road, his legs stretched out before him, and stared fixedly in the direction of the disappearing motor-car. He breathed short, his face wore a placid, satisfied expression, and at intervals he faintly murmured 'Poop-poop!'

The Mole was busy trying to quiet the horse, which he succeeded in doing after a time. Then he went to look at the cart, on its side in the ditch.

It was indeed a sorry sight. Panels and windows smashed, axles hopelessly bent, one wheel off, sardine-tins scattered over the wide world, and the bird in the bird-cage sobbing pitifully and calling to be let out.

The Rat came to help him, but their united efforts were not sufficient to right the cart. 'Hi! Toad!' they cried. 'Come and bear a hand, can't you!'

The Toad never answered a word, or budged from his seat in the road; so they went to see what was the matter with him. They found him in a sort of trance, a happy smile on his face, his eyes still fixed on the dusty wake of their destroyer. At intervals he was still heard to murmur 'Poop-poop!'

The Rat shook him by the shoulder. 'Are you coming to help us, Toad?' he demanded sternly.

'Glorious, stirring sight!' murmured Toad, never offering to move. 'The poetry of motion! The *real* way to travel! The *only* way to travel! Here today – in next week tomorrow! Villages skipped, towns and cities jumped – always somebody else's horizon! O bliss! O poop-poop! O my! O my!'

'O *stop* being an ass, Toad!' cried the Mole despairingly.

'And to think I never *knew*!' went on the Toad in a dreamy monotone. 'All those wasted years that lie behind me, I never knew, never even *dreamt*! But *now* – but now that I know, now that I fully realize! O what a flowery track lies spread before me, henceforth! What dust-clouds shall spring up behind me as I speed on my reckless way! What carts I shall fling carelessly into the ditch in the wake of my magnificent onset! Horrid little carts – common carts – canary-coloured carts!'

RUDYARD KIPLING

'The Elephant's Child'
FROM *Just So Stories*

ILLUSTRATED BY MICHAEL TERRY

In the High and Far-Off Times the Elephant, O Best Beloved, had no trunk. He had only a blackish, bulgy nose, as big as a boot, that he could wriggle about from side to side; but he couldn't pick up things with it. But there was one Elephant – a new Elephant – an Elephant's Child – who was full of 'satiable curtiosity, and that means he asked ever so many questions. *And* he lived in Africa, and he filled all Africa with his 'satiable curtiosities. He asked his tall aunt, the Ostrich, why her tail-feathers grew just so, and his tall aunt the Ostrich spanked him with her hard, hard claw. He asked his tall uncle, the Giraffe, what made his skin spotty, and his tall uncle, the Giraffe, spanked him with his hard, hard hoof. And still he was full of 'satiable curtiosity! He asked his broad aunt, the Hippopotamus, why her eyes were red, and his broad aunt, the Hippopotamus, spanked him with her broad, broad hoof; and he asked his hairy uncle, the Baboon, why melons tasted just so, and his hairy uncle, the Baboon, spanked him with his hairy, hairy paw. And still he was full of 'satiable curtiosity! He asked questions about everything that he saw, or heard, or felt, or smelt, or touched, and all his uncles and his aunts spanked him. And still he was full of 'satiable curtiosity!

One fine morning in the middle of the Precession of the Equinoxes this 'satiable Elephant's Child asked a new fine question that he had never asked before. He asked, 'What does the Crocodile have for dinner?' Then everybody said 'Hush!' in a loud and dretful tone, and they spanked him immediately and directly, without stopping, for a long time.

By and by, when that was finished, he came upon Kolokolo Bird sitting in the middle of a wait-a-bit thorn-bush, and he said, 'My father has spanked me, and my mother has spanked me; all my aunts and uncles have spanked me for my 'satiable curtiosity; and *still* I want to know what the Crocodile has for dinner!'

Then Kolokolo Bird said, with a mournful cry, 'Go to the banks of the great grey-green greasy Limpopo River, all set about with fever-trees, and find out.'

That very next morning, when there was nothing left of the

Equinoxes, because the Precession had preceded according to precedent, this 'satiable Elephant's Child took a hundred pounds of bananas (the little short red kind), and a hundred pounds of sugar-cane (the long purple kind), and seventeen melons (the greeny-crackly kind), and said to all his dear families, 'Goodbye. I am going to the great grey-green, greasy Limpopo River, all set about with fever-trees, to find out what the Crocodile has for dinner.' And they all spanked him once more for luck, though he asked them most politely to stop.

Then he went away, a little warm, but not at all astonished, eating melons, and throwing the rind about, because he could not pick it up.

He went from Graham's Town to Kimberley, and from Kimberley to Khama's Country, and from Khama's Country he went east by north, eating melons all the time, till at last he came to the banks of the great grey-green, greasy Limpopo River, all set about with fever-trees, precisely as Kolokolo Bird had said.

Now you must know and understand, O Best Beloved, that till that very week, and day, and hour, and minute, this 'satiable Elephant's Child had never seen a Crocodile, and did not know what one was like. It was all his 'satiable curtiosity.

The first thing that he found was a Bi-Coloured-Python-Rock-Snake curled round a rock.

''Scuse me,' said the Elephant's Child most politely, 'but have you seen such as thing as a Crocodile in these promiscuous parts?'

'*Have* I seen a Crocodile?' said the Bi-Coloured-Python-Rock-Snake, in a voice of dretful scorn. 'What will you ask me next?'

''Scuse me,' said the Elephant's Child, 'but could you kindly tell me what he has for dinner?'

Then the Bi-Coloured-Python-Rock-Snake uncoiled himself very quickly from the rock, and spanked the Elephant's Child with his scalesome, flailsome tail.

'That is odd,' said the Elephant's Child, 'because my father and my mother, and my uncle and my aunt, not to mention my other aunt, the Hippopotamus, and my other uncle, the Baboon, have all spanked me for my 'satiable curtiosity and I suppose this is the same thing.'

So he said goodbye very politely to the Bi-Coloured-Python-Rock-Snake, and helped to coil him up on the rock again, and went on, a little warm, but not at all astonished, eating melons, and throwing the rind about, because he could not pick it up, till he trod on what he thought was a log of wood at the very edge of the great grey-green, greasy Limpopo River, all set about with fever-trees.

But it was really the Crocodile, O Best Beloved, and the Crocodile winked one eye – like this!

''Scuse me,' said the Elephant's Child most politely, 'but do you happen to have seen a Crocodile in these promiscuous parts?'

Then the Crocodile winked the other eye, and lifted half his tail out of the mud; and the Elephant's Child stepped back most politely,

because he did not wish to be spanked again.

'Come hither, Little One,' said the Crocodile. 'Why do you ask such things?'

''Scuse me,' said the Elephant's Child most politely, 'but my father has spanked me, my mother has spanked me, not to mention my tall aunt, the Ostrich, and my tall uncle, the Giraffe, who can kick ever so hard, as well as my broad aunt, the Hippopotamus, and my hairy uncle, the Baboon, *and* including the Bi-Coloured-Python-Rock-Snake, with the scalesome, flailsome tail, just up the bank, who spanks harder than any of them; and *so,* if it's quite all the same to you, I don't want to be spanked any more.'

'Come hither, Little One,' said the Crocodile, 'for I am the Crocodile,' and he wept crocodile-tears to show it was quite true.

Then the Elephant's Child grew all breathless, and panted, and kneeled down on the bank and said, 'You are the very person I have been looking for all these long days. Will you please tell me what you have for dinner?'

'Come hither, Little One,' said the Crocodile, 'and I'll whisper.'

Then the Elephant's Child put his head down close to the Crocodile's musky, tusky mouth, and the Crocodile caught him by his little nose, which up to that very week, day, hour, and minute, had been no bigger than a boot, though much more useful.

'I think,' said the Crocodile — and he said it between his teeth, like this — 'I think today I will begin with Elephant's Child!'

At this, O Best Beloved, the Elephant's Child was much annoyed, and he said, speaking through his nose, like this, 'Led go! You are hurtig be!'

Then the Bi-Coloured-Python-Rock-Snake scuffled down from the bank and said, 'My young friend, if you do not now, immediately and instantly, pull as hard as ever you can, it is my opinion that your acquaintance in the large-pattern leather ulster' (and by this he meant the Crocodile) 'will jerk you into yonder limpid stream before you can say Jack Robinson.'

This is the way Bi-Coloured-Python-Rock-Snakes always talk.

Then the Elephant's Child sat back on his little haunches, and pulled, and pulled, and pulled, and his nose began to stretch. And the Crocodile floundered into the water, making it all creamy with great sweeps of his tail, and *he* pulled, and pulled, and pulled.

And the Elephant's Child's nose kept on stretching; and the Elephant's Child spread all his little four legs and pulled, and pulled, and pulled, and his nose kept on stretching; and the Crocodile threshed his tail like an oar, and *he* pulled, and pulled, and pulled, and at each pull the Elephant's Child's nose grew longer and longer – and it hurt him hijjus!

Then the Elephant's Child felt his legs slipping, and he said through his nose, which was now nearly five feet long, 'This is too butch for be!'

Then the Bi-Coloured-Python-Rock-Snake came down from the bank, and knotted himself in a double-clovehitch round the Elephant's Child's hind-legs, and said, 'Rash and inexperienced traveller, we will now seriously devote ourselves to a little high tension, because if we do not, it is my impression that yonder self-propelling man-of-war with the armour-plated upper deck' (and by this, O Best Beloved, he meant the Crocodile) 'will permanently vitiate your future career.'

That is the way all Bi-Coloured-Python-Rock-Snakes always talk.

So he pulled, and the Elephant's Child pulled, and the Crocodile pulled; but the Elephant's Child and the Bi-Coloured-Python-Rock-Snake pulled hardest; and at last the Crocodile let go of the Elephant's Child's nose with a plop that you could hear all up and down the Limpopo.

Then the Elephant's Child sat down most hard and sudden; but first he was careful to say 'Thank you' to the Bi-Coloured-Python-Rock-Snake; and next he was kind to his poor pulled nose, and wrapped it all up in cool banana leaves, and hung it in the grey-green, greasy Limpopo to cool.

'What are you doing that for?' said the Bi-Coloured-Python-Rock-Snake.

''Scuse me,' said the Elephant's Child, 'but my nose is badly out of shape, and I am waiting for it to shrink.'

'Then you will have to wait a long time,' said the Bi-Coloured-Python-Rock-Snake. 'Some people do not know what is good for them.'

The Elephant's Child sat there for three days waiting for his nose to shrink. But it never grew any shorter, and, besides, it made him squint. For, O Best Beloved, you will see and understand that the Crocodile had pulled it out into a really truly trunk same as all Elephants have today.

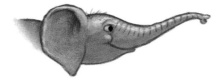

INDEX OF AUTHORS

BIOGRAPHICAL NOTES

RICHARD ADAMS was born in Berkshire. Until 1974 he worked in the Civil Service and rose to Assistant Secretary in the Department of the Environment. *Watership Down* (1972) and his two other novels involving animals, *Shardik* (1974) and *The Plague Dogs* (1977), were written both for children and adults.

B. B. (1905–1990) is the pen-name of D. J. (Denys James) Watkins-Pitchford, born in Northamptonshire. From 1930 to 1947 he taught art at Rugby School and illustrated his books under his real name. *The Little Grey Men* (1942) won the Carnegie Medal. Other books include *Brendon Chase* (1944) and *The Wizard of Boland* (1959).

RICHMAL CROMPTON (1890–1969) was born in Lancashire. She taught Classics until 1924 when she contracted polio. A writer for both adults and children, she is famed for the William books which, beginning with *Just William* (1922), comprise thirty-eight titles in all.

ROALD DAHL (1916–1990) was born in Glamorgan, Wales, of Norwegian parents. He is best known for his highly successful books for children, including *Charlie and the Chocolate Factory* (1967), *The BFG* (1982), *The Witches* (1983) and *Matilda* (1989).

ANNE FINE was born in 1947 in Leicester. Humour features strongly in her children's novels, which include *The Stone Menagerie* (1980) and *The Granny Project* (1983). *Goggle-Eyes* (1990) won the Carnegie Medal.

KENNETH GRAHAME (1859–1932) was born in Edinburgh, but from the age of five, when his mother died, he grew up in Berkshire. He became an official of the Bank of England. Early titles include *The Golden Age* (1895) and *Dream Days* (1898) but it is *The Wind in the Willows* (1908) that has become a classic.

RUSSELL HOBAN was born in 1925 in Pennsylvania. Since 1969 he has lived in London. He has written a number of picture books, including *How Tom Beat Captain Najork and His Hired Sportsmen* (1974) and *The Dancing Tigers* (1979). *The Mouse and His Child* was published in 1967.

TED HUGHES (1930–1998) was born in Yorkshire. He became Poet Laureate in 1984. His writing for children includes the verse–collection *Season Songs* (1975) and the stories of *How the Whale Became* (1963), *The Iron Man* (1968) and *Tales of the Early World* (1988).

DICK KING-SMITH was born in 1922 in Gloucestershire. He was a farmer and later a primary school teacher before he began to write for children. His stories include *The Sheep-Pig* (1983), *Noah's Brother* (1986), *The Water Horse* (1990) and many titles for early readers, including *E.S.P.* (1987).

RUDYARD KIPLING (1865–1936) was born in Bombay of English parents. From 1899 he lived most of his life in England as a full-time writer, receiving the Nobel Prize for Literature in 1907. His classic books for children are *The Jungle Book* (1894), *Kim* (1901) and the *Just So Stories* (1902).

C. S. (CLIVE STAPLES) LEWIS (1898–1963) was born in Belfast. He was a distinguished literary scholar and taught at Oxford until 1954, when he became Professor of Medieval and Renaissance Literature at Cambridge. For children he wrote his sequence of seven fantasy novels, *The Chronicles of Narnia* (1950–1956), of which the first is *The Lion, the Witch and the Wardrobe*.

PENELOPE LIVELY was born in 1933 in Cairo. She came to England in 1945 to attend boarding-school and subsequently settled here. Her novels for children include *The Ghost of Thomas Kempe* (1973) and *The House at Norham Gardens* (1974). She also writes fiction for adults and *Moon Tiger* (1987) won the Booker Prize.

JOHN MASEFIELD (1878–1967) was born in Herefordshire. At fifteen he went to sea and it was *Salt-Water Ballads* (1902) that established him as a writer. He became Poet Laureate in 1930. He also wrote fantasy fiction, including two classics for children, *The Midnight Folk* (1927) and its sequel *The Box of Delights* (1935).

JENNY NIMMO was born in 1944 in Berkshire. She worked for the BBC from 1964 to 1975, when she became a full-time writer. The landscape and legends of Wales, where she lives, feature in her stories for children, which include *The Snow Spider* (1982) and *The Red Secret* (1989).

MARY NORTON was born in 1903 in London. She lived in Portugal and then in New York, where her first book *The Magic Bed-Knob* (1943) was published. In *The Borrowers* (1952), which won the Carnegie Medal, she created a race of tiny people who have reappeared in several sequels, the last being *The Borrowers Avenged* (1982).

JILL PATON WALSH was born in 1937 in London. She began to write after she gave up her work as an English teacher in 1962. She has published several historical novels, including *The Emperor's Winding Sheet* (1974) and other titles include *A Parcel of Patterns* (1983) and *Gaffer Samson's Luck* (1984).

PHILIPPA PEARCE was born in 1920 in Cambridgeshire. She worked for BBC Schools Radio and in children's publishing before becoming a full-time writer in 1959. *Tom's Midnight Garden* (1958) won the Carnegie Medal. Other notable books are *A Dog So Small* (1962) and *The Way to Sattin Shore* (1983).

TERRY PRATCHETT was born in 1948 in Buckinghamshire. He worked as a journalist and for the CEGB (Central Electricity Generating Board) before becoming a full-time writer. His first book, *The Carpet People,* was published in 1971. He is most famously known for his *Discworld* novels which have a worldwide cult following. In 1998 he was awarded an OBE.

NOEL STREATFEILD (1895–1986) was born in Sussex. She was an actress during the 1920s, but then turned to writing adult fiction. Her first book for children, *Ballet Shoes* (1936), initiated a vogue for career novels. Her other books include *The Circus is Coming* (1938), which won the Carnegie Medal.

J. R. R. (JOHN RONALD REUEL) TOLKIEN (1892–1973) was born in South Africa and came to England when he was three. From 1925 to 1959 he was a Professor in the field of Anglo-Saxon at Oxford. During the 1960s *The Hobbit* (1937) and its epic sequel *The Lord of the Rings* (1954, 1955) achieved world-wide fame.

SYLVIA WAUGH was born in 1935 in Gateshead. She taught English Literature for twenty years. After retiring, she wrote *The Mennyms* (1993) which won the *Guardian* Award for Children's Fiction. *The Mennyms* was followed by *Mennyms in the Wilderness*, *Mennyms Under Siege*, *Mennyms Alone* and *Mennyms Alive*.

E. B. (ELWYN BROOKS) WHITE (1899–1985) was born in New York. He was a humorous essayist well known for his contributions to *The New Yorker*. He published three books for children: *Stuart Little* (1945), *Charlotte's Web* (1952) and *The Trumpet of the Swan* (1970).

JACQUELINE WILSON was born in 1945 in Bath. She had her first story published when she was seventeen and was a journalist for several years before taking up writing full-time. She has now written over thirty children's books including *Mark Spark in the Dark* (1993), *Double Act* (1995) winner of the Smarties Book Prize and the Children's Book Award, *Bad Girls* (1996) and *The Lottie Project* (1997).

ACKNOWLEDGEMENTS

The publisher gratefully acknowledges the following for permission to reproduce copyright material in this book.

Watership Down copyright © Richard Adams, 1972, reprinted by permission of David Higham Associates; *The Little Grey Men* copyright © B. B., 1942, reprinted by permission of David Higham Associates; *Just William* copyright © Richmal Crompton, 1922, reprinted by permission of Macmillan Publishers Ltd; *Charlie and the Chocolate Factory* copyright © Roald Dahl, 1964, reprinted by permission of David Higham Associates and Penguin Books Ltd; *Flour Babies* copyright © Anne Fine, 1992, reprinted by permission of Penguin Books Ltd; *The Wind in the Willows* by Kenneth Grahame, 1908, copyright © The University Chest, Oxford, reproduced by permission of Curtis Brown, London; *The Mouse and His Child* copyright © Russell Hoban, 1967, reprinted by permission of Faber and Faber Ltd., 1969 and HarperCollins Publishers Ltd; *The Iron Man* copyright © Ted Hughes, 1968, reprinted by permission of Faber and Faber Ltd; *The Sheep-Pig* copyright © Dick King-Smith, 1983, reprinted by permission of Penguin Books Ltd; 'The Elephant's Child' by Rudyard Kipling taken from *Just So Stories*, 1902, copyright © Rudyard Kipling, reproduced by permission of A P Watt Ltd on behalf of The National Trust for places of Historic Interest or Natural Beauty; *The Lion, the Witch and the Wardrobe* copyright © C. S. Lewis, 1950, reprinted by permission of HarperCollins Publishers Ltd; *The Ghost of Thomas Kempe* copyright © Penelope Lively, 1973, reprinted by permission of Heinemann Young Books, a division of Egmont Children's Books; *The Box of Delights* copyright © John Masefield, 1935, reproduced by permission of The Society of Authors as the Literary Representative of the Estate of John Masefield; *The Snow Spider* copyright © Jenny Nimmo, 1986, published in the UK by Methuen Children's Books and Mammoth, imprints of Egmont Children's Books Limited, London and used with permission; *The Borrowers* copyright © Mary Norton, 1952, reprinted by permission of Orion Children's Books; *Gaffer Samson's Luck* copyright © Jill Paton Walsh, 1984, reprinted by permission of David Higham Associates; *Tom's Midnight Garden* copyright © Philippa Pearce, 1958, reprinted by permission of Oxford University Press; *Diggers* copyright © Terry and Lyn Pratchett, 1990, published by Doubleday and reprinted by permission of Transworld Publishers Ltd; *Ballet Shoes* copyright © Noel Streatfeild, 1936, reprinted by permission of Orion Children's Books; *The Hobbit* copyright © J. R. R. Tolkien, 1937, reprinted by permission of HarperCollins Publishers Ltd; *The Mennyms* copyright © Sylvia